Nymphopervtress

The Desiree Logan Story

Rachelle Jarred

Nymphopervtress Copyright and Disclaimer

DEDICATION

This is my first book and I wanna dedicate to a few people. First off, and foremost, I wanna thank God for giving me the talent to creatively put my thoughts in writing. Secondly my two children Sha'niya and Antonio Jr. for letting me be in my little zone and stay focused. My best friend Shawntia for being the good friend that she is no matter what she says. And last, but not the least, my friend Ivan. If it wasn't for him, I would have never got my mind back on my dream of becoming an author. Without these people in my life, I don't know where I would be. I love them to the moon and back.

Contents

Prologue

"Aahhh! Oh my God!" I yelled loudly. I was under a dark figure that was giving me the "business" just how I like it. I called him that because that's exactly what he was. A dark figure.

We had only met a few short hours ago at a nightclub. No introductions required. I let him take me back to his house instead of mine. No need for false hope. I never wanted to nor was I going to see him again.

When we both had finally climaxed, I reached for my phone to check my messages. None. So I did what I normally did in this situation. I reached for my purse and pulled out my wipes. He was too busy trying to regain his composure to notice what I was doing. By the time he turned my way, I was fully dressed and grabbing my jean jacket from the floor.

"Hey, where are you going?"

"Home," I replied.

"I thought we could go again or at least wake up together in the morning."

I looked at him and rolled my eyes.

"Yeah, about that, I don't think that is gonna happen. I got what I wanted so now I'm ready to jet. "

"What the fuck? If I had known you were a hoe then I would've let my boys come with me," he laughed.

I laughed with him. "Well you know what they say: Ain't no fun unless the homies get some too. But, oh well, I'm outta here whatever your name is."

I turned my back and walked out towards the front door. Following me were all types of "bitches" "hoes" "sluts"; everything I have been called a million times before.

Did I care? Fuck no. Did it make me laugh? Hell yeah. I was used to niggas saying the same shit to me when we finished fucking. It didn't bother me at all.

My name is Desiree Michelle Logan and this is the life I lived…

Nymphopervtress

Chapter One
The Beginning

♛

It was a bright and hot ass summer day out in D.C. I was both excited and mad. I was happy because I could go outside without a jacket on or anything, but mad because it was eight in the morning and seventy degrees out!

I reached over and grabbed my phone. Two missed calls and fifteen messages. What the fuck?! was all that ran through my mind. Damn! I hope nothing bad happened. I checked the messages and they were all from my boyfriend, Jay.

Ah, Jay, has been my boyfriend for the past five months. He was, well, Jay. Nothing really special there. Tall, slim, redbone, low cut, fresh-to-death dude. Not even close to my type. I think it was his white and gold Lexus that caught my eye. Maybe it was his sexy eyes. Or maybe it was his nice house. Hell, I don't know.

I met Jay when I was walking home from school one day. And if I haven't classified it yet, I'm only seventeen. Yeah, that's right. Seventeen, but looked like a grown woman. I had C-cup breasts, a small waist, and a nice round ass. However, I always kept it covered. I was a "plain Jane" you could say. But, anyway, back to Jay.

I had just split from my girlfriends and was walking down the alley from Rosedale towards my apartment complex. I had my headphones on listening to a Project Pat cd when this beautiful car pulled up beside me. I instantly got nervous until the driver window rolled down. That eased my nervousness, a little anyway.

I looked at the driver without saying anything. He spoke first.

"What's up with you, Sexy?"

I looked behind me as I stood there stiffened. No way was he talking to me.

"What you looking around for, Baby," he laughed.

"I was trynna figure out who you were talking to. You damn sure not talking to me."

"And why can't I be talking to you?" he asked as he looked me up and down. I wasn't dressed like much. I had on some Parasuco jeans, some Reebok classics, and rocking some straight back cornrows. Who the hell did this dude think he was fooling?

"What's your name? I don't wanna be talking to a stranger," I said looking up and down the alley.

"My name is Jay and yours?"

"Desiree," I said extending my hand towards him. He took it and kissed it. All I could do was roll my eyes.

"So, Ms. Desiree, do you have a man, sweetheart?"

"Uh,no. I go to school with boys and they not even close to being men the way they act."

"That's good to know. Well, can I be-"

I cut him off before he could even continue. "I don't have a boyfriend because I'm seventeen and all I'm worried about are sports and school."

He looked at me funny. "You only seventeen, baby? You're a baby for real. Well check this out. Take my number and give me a call if you want to."

He wrote his number down and handed it to me. I took it, shoved it in my pocket, threw my headphones back on and walked off. I called him that next night. Everything was history after that.

I called Jay back because I didn't know what the hell his problem was. All his messages were the same. "Where are you?" "You better not be with a nigga." "Call me back, Boo." "What kind of games are you playing?" All I could do was shake my head.

As soon as he answered the phone, he went off. "Bitch, where the fuck you at?!" he yelled.

"Nigga I'm in the fuck-"

"Lil' girl you better watch your damn mouth. Ain't no niggas on this motherfucking phone, aight? I don't know what the fuck your problem is but don't get fucked up. Now I'm gonna ask your ass one more time. Where. The fuck. Are you?"

"Baby, calm down."

"Don't fucking say shit else. All I wanna hear out your mouth is where the fuck you are."

I took a deep breath and told him I was in the house.

"Bring your ass outside. Now," he said coldly.

I looked out the window and this nigga was outside my building. I knew I had better hurry up if I didn't wanna get cussed out anymore. So I ran outside with my socks and my pajamas on. When I stepped out the building, I gave him a hug and a kiss. He didn't even seem like the same nigga that was just on the phone a few minutes ago seeing how calm he was. We walked to the car and we drove around because he said we needed to talk. Oh goodness.

Nymphopervtress

"You know I really like you, Desiree," he said. I remained silent and nodded my head. "You open your fucking mouth when I'm talking to you."

"Sorry, Baby. Yes I know you like me. But what's wrong?"

Before I knew it, he slapped the shit out of me. I was stuck. No retaliation or nothing.

"Sorry, but I had to do it. You need to be kept in check. I'm the man. You don't ask me no damn questions. Now, I'm stressed and I need to relieve it." I looked at him oddly. "What I mean is, I need some pussy. So what's up?" he parked the car behind an abandoned school.

I sat there sobbing before I answered. "What do you want me to do, Jay? I mean, I have never had sex before, remember? I'm still a virgin."

"I know and I want to be your first. I will make your first time memorable, Shorty, believe that. So what do you say?"

"Um, well, I guess."

"What you mean you guess? Who else would do it? I'm your man and that's my job. I mean, those little niggas you go to school with don't know what the hell to do but I do."

"Sure, Baby," I said after thinking it over. "When do you wanna do it?"

"Be ready in a week."

"Okay."

We drove back to my apartment complex in silence. He kissed me deeply before I stepped out the car. It felt weird and I looked at him crazily.

"What's wrong?" he asked blankly.

"You hit me for what reason, Jay?"

"I told you I was stressed."

"So what that gotta do with me?"

"You part of the reason and you need to fix it before it happens again. I don't wanna hear nothing else about it, girl. As a matter of fact, don't even call me. I will call you next week and you better answer the phone. Got me?"

"Yes, Jay," I said as I exited the car.

So many thoughts ran through my mind as I slowly walked back in the house. What did I just get myself into? Nobody outside my family has ever hit me before. Should I tell my mother? No. I couldn't tell anybody.

He was twenty-three. I was seventeen. He would definitely go to jail. I sucked it up and pushed it to the back of my mind.

You know what they say: "forgive but never forget."

****

The next few days of school was one big blur. I was distracted from what Jay had said about him being my first. Deep down I wanted him to be, but I wasn't ready. How does one prepare for something like this? I didn't know because I never thought about it. I wanted to wait until I got married, but I didn't want to lose Jay. I decided to do it. I was going to give myself to Jay tomorrow. Damn! Wednesday got here fast as shit, I thought to myself.

"Oooh, mommy," I called to my mother Denise. She came in the room soon after.

"Why you not up for school?"

"I don't feel good, ma. Can I stay home today, please?"

"You look fine to me, nigga," she said. I tried to hold back my laughter by getting back under my blanket.

"Oh my goodness, ma, please. You know if I felt good I woulda been up. I'm serious, mommy."

She looked at me strangely. "Whatever, girl. I'm about to go to work. I should be home around five-thirty at the latest. Call me if you need anything."

"Ok, mommy," I said from under the cover. I can't believe that worked. As soon as I heard the door close, I called Jay.

"Hey, Baby," I sang into the phone as soon as he answered.

"What's up?"

"Are you on the way?"

"Yeah. I should be there in thirty."

"Ok. I'll be ready."

"Cool."

Now what do I wear? I didn't have any girly clothes. All I had were jeans and sweats. I chose to wear a tank top and a pair of track pants that I always wore to cheerleading practice. By the time I finished brushing my teeth and fixing my ponytail, he was calling my phone to let me know he was outside.

We rode in the car to his house, not saying anything. My palms were sweaty from me being so nervous. I guess he called himself trying to ease the nervousness by kissing my hand and holding it the rest of the way to his spot.

We pulled up to a quiet neighborhood with attractive, yet simple- looking townhouses. We walked into his and instantly went upstairs to his bedroom. We started kissing as soon as we got in there. He backed me up to the bed and continued to kiss me as we got on the bed. He was on top of me. Kissing my lips. Kissing my neck. My heart, however, was beating loud and rapidly.

He was still kissing on my neck as he slipped his hand down in my pants. I froze.

"It's okay, Baby. I'm gonna be gentle with you," he said with soft eyes looking down at me. I just nodded my head in agreement. He was rubbing my pussy trying to get it "wet" as he said. He tried to push a finger inside me and it hurt. He told me it was supposed to.

I guess I had gotten wet because he reached for a condom and put it on after he took his basketball shorts off. He was ready but I wasn't. I looked at his penis and got scared of it. He got on top and tried to push it in and it hurt like fuck! I made him stop and he got upset but he didn't hit me.

"I thought you was ready, Desi?"

"I thought I was too but I'm not, Jay. That shit hurts and I don't wanna do it."

He looked down at me and shook his head but said he understood. We both put our clothes back on. He drove me home and all the while sitting in silence. It was awkward but I didn't care.

When we got back around my way, he sternly told me, "Don't call me no more with your games, slim. When you grow the fuck up then u call a nigga."

I didn't even respond to his ass. I got out the car and went into the house and laid down. In my mind, I thought, I'm glad I didn't fuck him. I will save it for somebody else. I went to sleep with a smile on my face because I knew I wasn't going to call him ever again. And I was fine with that.

Chapter Two
The Move

My mom got home and sat me and my little sister, Monet, down. "Well, I have some good news and bad news. We're gonna be moving this weekend," she said excitedly. I looked at her, puzzled.

"So, um, what's the good news? I mean, what else is new? We're always moving," I yelled.

"I don't know who in the hell you think you talking to but I will knock your ass into the middle of next week if you don't calm your ass down! I don't know what the hell is wrong with you ungrateful ass kids."

Monet just had to chime in with her cents. "I'm glad to be moving, mommy. Can we move today?" she asked enthusiastically.

"Well, we can start packing now. So go get y'all stuff together while I do the rest."

I dragged my feet as I walked to the room I shared with my baby sister. I packed my stuff up slowly as I held back tears. My mom's decision to move to Maryland was final. What the hell made her wanna do that? Did she think about us? What about school? What about my friends? I didn't wanna go to a new school and meet new people all over again. That shit sucked! I was tired of this moving shit.

****

Well it's Friday and everything is finally packed and we are already withdrawn from school. My friends and I already said our goodbyes and shared a long group hug. I was really gonna miss my crew.

****

We finally got settled in our new apartment and our new schools. I hated it! I missed my old school. My friends. Even my teachers. Hell, I was even missing Jay's crazy ass.

I wondered what he was doing. Was he missing me? Was he even thinking about me? Probably not. He probably picked up another virgin by now. Maybe somebody more experienced. I should give him a call tonight.

It was my first day at this new school. Central High. The administrators had already pissed me off today. And only a few short moments ago I was close to getting in a fight just because of the neighborhood I was from. That shit was crazy but it didn't escalate. That dude knew he didn't want that work. That same day I made a new friend named Jessica.

She came up to me at my locker and introduced herself to me. "Hey, you're new here, aren't you?"

"What gave it away?" I responded sarcastically.

She cleared her throat. "Well, I knew already. If you need a friend, I'm here. I'm Jessica. What's your name?"

"Desiree but everyone calls me Desi."

"Nice to meet you. What class do you have now?"

"My favorite subject. Lunch," I said and we both laughed.

"That's cool. That's my favorite too and it's time for me to go feed my belly too," Jessica responded as she rubbed her belly. This girl was nuts but I liked her so far.

We walked into the cafeteria and stood in line. I was hungry as hell and they were serving pizza for lunch. The line was moving and then it stopped. I scanned the crowded cafeteria. It was a lot of goddamn teens in here and it seemed like everybody were in cliques. Suddenly, my eyes landed on this one girl. She looked good but looked like a dude. She had to be a Dom. Why was I fascinated by her? I liked boys not girls. Or was it the other way around? Was it possible to be attracted to both?

My panties instantly got wet. What the hell? How is that possible? I couldn't believe this was happening right in the cafeteria. Around all these damn people. I noticed her walking towards me and Jessica. Oh no.

"What's up, Jessica?"

"Hey, Shannon. This is Desiree. She's new here."

She looked me up and down. It felt like she was undressing me with her eyes. Nervously, I managed to say "hello."

"How you doing?" she asked, licking her lips.

"I'm fine," I responded not trying to make eye contact.

"Yes you are."

"Hey cut it out, Shannon," Jessica laughed. "Don't scare her off already."

"Nah, it's cool. Nothing but love here. But aye, Imma check y'all later. See you in next period."

Nymphopervtress

"See ya."

Jessica and I got our lunch and sat down. She gave me the rundown on the students, teachers, and about herself. Damn that girl could talk. We found out that all our classes are together except trigonometry. Before I knew it, lunch was over and we were headed to gym class—one of my least favorite subjects.

I was kind of happy that we shared most of our classes. At least I wasn't alone on this journey. We got to the gym and our teacher, Ms. Bayou, gathered everybody together.

"Okay, ladies and gents, we have a new student joining us today. Her name is Desiree Logan and I want you all to welcome her."

I looked around at everyone and they were all staring back at me. I didn't like being the center of attention. "Hey, everybody. You all can call me, Desi."

"Would you like to share with us about yourself?"

In my head I wanted to say, "Yeah, I wanna share myself with y'all." Hell, my teacher was hot and she was making me hot. "Well, I'm seventeen and I just moved from DC with my mom and my little sister. What else? Oh yeah. I like to exercise."

"Well that's great," Ms. Bayou responded. "In that case, everybody in the locker rooms. Put on your gym clothes and be out here in ten minutes," she said. She blew her whistle and everybody split up. I walked in the locker room and gulped.

Females were just standing around without shirts or pants on like they were in the comfort of their own home. Just naked. Naked as the day they were born. My mouth started to salivate as I scanned the room. Big breasts, little breasts, and all those asses surrounding me. I couldn't take it. I quickly went into a stall, changed my clothes, and got back to the gym. Again, my panties were wet.

So I made it through gym class. It was finally the last period of the day. I walked into my math class and it was damn near empty. It was only like five females, including myself, and like eight guys. They looked like a nerdy bunch. All except for one dude in particular.

He was off to the last row of seats near the window. Brown skin, shoulder length dreads, and looked like he had hazel eyes. He was handsome yet kind of creepy for some reason. I decided to find a seat in the corner away from him so I can watch him from afar.

After forty-five minutes of learning about trigonometry, school was finally over for the day. I got my bag and rushed to my locker. I grabbed my

English book out and left the school with quickness. I wanted to hurry and get home so I could call Jay.

When I got home, my mom was busy in the kitchen and Monet was watching TV. I tried to speed walk past the kitchen but my mother had seen me.

"So, how was your first day?"

"It was cool. I met a girl. Two girls actually."

"See. Making new friends already."

"Yep," I responded ending the conversation as I walked away. I picked up the cordless phone on the way to my room because I had to charge my cell phone. I sat down on the bed and just held the phone. What if he didn't even wanna talk to me? I debated calling him now. I just held the phone and stared at it. Fuck it! I thought. I'm gonna call. The worst he can do is not answer. Here goes nothing. I dialed his number and it rang three times before he answered.

"Hey, Jay," I said as pleasantly as possible.

"What?" he barked.

Maybe this wasn't gonna be as easy as I thought. "I miss you, baby. We moved to Maryland and I don't like it one bit. I'm not liking not seeing or hearing your voice either," I cooed.

"Mmhmm. So what does that mean?"

I got silent and took a deep breath. "It means I wanna see you. I'm ready to give myself to you."

"Why now all of a sudden?"

"I've just been having all these sexual thoughts and now I'm ready for the real thing."

"When?"

"I can sneak out tonight. What time will you be here?"

"Be outside at eleven."

"Ok."

"Ok."

It was about to be on. It was gonna be my birthday tomorrow and I was about to enjoy a great birthday gift. Jay was gonna be my first after all.

Nymphopervtress

Chapter Three:
Getting Down To Business

I went outside a few minutes before eleven. I was so nervous about sneaking out the house. I have never done anything like this before. But if I had to risk getting in trouble to make my body feel good, then what the hell. Nothing was gonna stand in my way.

Jay got there at eleven exactly. I got in the car and we both sat there.

"Are you sure you're ready to do this, Desiree?"

"Yes I do. My birthday is in an hour and I can't think of anything more special to do to bring my birthday in."

"Alright. You know I'm gonna make sure it's special for you, so don't worry."

"Ok," I replied. He pulled off and I sat back with my eyes closed. I inhaled his Curve cologne and exhaled slowly. I loved that cologne.

Instead of going to his house, we detoured and went to a hotel. We parked in the parking lot of The Hampton Inn. We went into the room and my heart stopped.

He had soft music playing and the lights were dim. He had white rose petals on the bed. It looked like a scene right out of a movie. I was in awe. He walked up behind me and started kissing the back of my neck. It felt so good. He started to feel on my body. He cupped my breasts and pinched my nipples. I let out a whimper and sounded like a puppy.

My body got hotter when he started rubbing my clit through my pants. I started to grind my plump ass against his jeans. I felt his dick get hard through his pants. He was getting turned on and so was I.

"Are you ready?" he whispered in my ear. I couldn't even answer him, so I just nodded.

He turned me around towards him and kissed me passionately. He took my shirt off and sucked on my breasts. He squeezed and pinched and bit my nipples. That shit was feeling so good my damn knees started to feel like jelly. I started to kiss him back roughly and we headed towards the bed; all the while removing our clothes. We got to the bed and stopped.

I climbed into the bed and got under the covers. He grabbed a condom off the nightstand and I watched as he put it on his erect penis. He got under the covers and got on top of me.

"This is only gonna hurt for a few seconds. I promise you, Baby."

"Okay, Baby."

He pressed the head of his penis against my vagina. It hurt for more than a second. I felt a lot of pressure then it stopped. He had popped my cherry.

"You good?" he asked after he got in.

"Yes," I whispered softly.

"Good. You a big girl now, Baby. Let daddy take care of you."

He stroked my pussy with his dick and it was feeling amazing. I had forgotten all about the pain I was in. It felt like I was in heaven now. We both moaned and groaned. He kept kissing me and telling me that he loved me and how happy he was to be my first. I listened to everything. It all sounded good. Everything was feeling good.

He started to pound my pussy a little harder and going a little more deeper. I couldn't take it anymore. I felt something warm and sticky between my thighs. I had just experienced my first orgasm. Moments later, he ejaculated too.

He rolled off top of me and laid next to me. He pulled me over to him and I laid my head on his chest.

"So how did you like it?" he asked, as he rubbed my back.

"It was nice. I enjoyed it. Every minute of it."

"That's what's up. You wanna go again?" he asked and we both laughed.

"Yeah. But in a different position."

"What position?"

I didn't even answer him. I just stroked his penis until it got back stiff and gently eased myself on top. I slid slowly down his shaft and it felt like I just put the end of a baseball bat inside my pussy. I started to move my hips back and forth and kissed him as I rode. I did everything I saw them do on the pornos I watched. I rode and moaned as he laid on his back and made sounds that matched mine. Before I knew it, we had simultaneously climaxed again. I collapsed on top of him and he held me. We drifted off to sleep and I couldn't think of anything else right now except this life-changing event.

I'm not sure what time we fell asleep or how long we had been asleep. All I know is that we were awakened when my alarm went off at 6:45 a.m.—ike it did every weekday morning.

I woke up and looked around the room. Oh shit. I forgot I wasn't home. But I had to get my ass there before my mother got up at 7:30.

I hurried and woke Jay up as I rushed to get dressed. He jumped up and got dressed too. We grabbed our phones and we ran out the hotel room.

We got in the car and sped to my house. We pulled up and he gave me a kiss along with a small box before I jumped out the car.

To my surprise my mom wasn't even home. Damn! I dodged that bullet. I went in the house and hopped in the shower after I stripped out of my clothes. I washed all over my body but I just kept touching myself. It felt good to explore my body. I got out the shower and went into the room to get dressed. I got dressed quickly. I remembered the box that Jay had given me and I opened it. It was a small necklace with a pendant on it that read 'JD' on it. I put it on and looked myself over in the floor length mirror I had on the back of my door. I wonder if I looked any different. Only time would tell.

There were only two things on my mind: getting some more dick and who's dick was it gonna be.

Chapter Four:
Let The Frenzy Begin

All day at school, I have been thinking about sex. Sex with Jay. Sex with any attractive person I saw at school that day. This was so weird, but I was enjoying imagining me and others getting busy. This has been a long day and I still had three more hours to go. I was headed to gym class when Shannon walked up to me and threw her arm across my shoulders. I shuttered as if a cold wind had just hit me.

"Hey, Boo, what's up?" she said.

"Boo? Who you calling, Boo?" I asked smiling at her.

"You my Boo," she replied as she moved her hand down to the small of my back.

"What's up, Shannon?"

"Well, me and you, I hope," she replied. I looked at her with a weird look. "Not like that, ma. I meant like we can hangout and chill. A bunch of us are going out to the movies to see Superbad. You in?"

I thought about it for a second. It would be a good way to meet some new people. "Sure, I can come. When are y'all going?"

"Tonight. It's Friday, so the movies stay open a little later. You don't have a curfew do you?" she asked laughing.

Truth is, I didn't actually have a set curfew. I never went anywhere to have a curfew. "No, I don't," I said. I hadn't even realized that we walked right past the gymnasium. We were at the end of the hall where nobody could see us. Out of nowhere, Shannon kissed me on the cheek.

"Shannon! What the hell?" I yelled at her. It was a simple quick peck on the cheek. I liked it but I didn't wanna let her know I did.

"My bad. I thought you wanted me to."

"Look, if you wanted to kiss me then all you had to do was this," I replied, as I grabbed her by her shirt and kissed her lips roughly; tongue and all. She held me around my waist as I held her around her neck. We broke our kiss when we heard somebody fall into the gym doors.

We looked at each other strangely, then walked back towards the gym. Luckily, we weren't late. So we just hurried to change and go back out on the floor to do our "suicides." The entire time, all I could think about was Shannon. That kiss was the best I have ever experienced. The first time I have ever kissed a female and I enjoyed it more than kissing a man. Even more than kissing Jay. Oh my god! I forgot about Jay. We had something special. How could I do that to him? That's all I thought about as I headed to the locker room.

I went into the locker room and took a shower. My mind was so far gone that I didn't even notice Shannon come up by the curtain. I jumped.

"What's up, Shannon?"

"Nothing. Just making sure you were alright."

"I'm good, but look. That was a mistake. We never should have kissed. I don't want that to interfere with us being friends or anything," I rambled on for a few more minutes until she put her hand over my mouth to shut me up.

"Calm down, Desi. It's all good, Boo. We were just caught up in the moment, that's all. It was good though," she said laughing. I smiled at her.

"Cool. Well, let me get back to my shower so I can get my ass ready for my last class."

"Aight then. We gon' link up later. Don't forget."

"I'm not," I replied and she walked off. I finished up my shower and headed to math class.

Again, that same boy was in the corner again today. I decided to sit by him today. We were doing exponents and shit in class today. I didn't know what the hell to do. Luckily, we partnered up and he was mine. His name was Scott.

"Just let me give you all the answers," he said to me. Did he think I was an idiot or something? I mean math wasn't my strongest subject but I did know a little. But hey, if he wanted to do the work then I was gonna let him.

"Is that like a macho thing? I mean, I can do it myself but I could use a little help."

"That's cool. I'm gonna walk you through the problems and breakdown how I get the answer. I already know he gonna give us this shit for homework," we both laughed but it was true.

"Cool." We did the ten problems and he showed me how he got the answers just like he said he would. He was so smart. I even answered a few myself. We were so close I could smell his scent. He used old spice body wash or cologne. My pussy started to wake up so I had to shift in my seat. He looked at me oddly and I just smiled.

"Are you okay, Desiree?"

"Yeah, I am. And please call me, Desi."

"How about I call you tonight?"

"What?" I responded. I clearly heard what the hell he asked me. I just wanted him to repeat it.

"Can I call you later?"

I thought about it. It would be okay to talk to him on the phone, right? I mean he was a classmate and all. "Yeah, you can call me. I may need your help with this work," I playfully laughed.

"Well in that case how about I come over after school and we work together again."

"That's fine. Meet me at my locker on the first floor after class."

The bell went off ten minutes later. Scott left before me and went to his locker. I headed to mine and saw Jessica and Shannon standing at theirs. "What's up, y'all?"

"Nothing much," Jessica said. "That bitch, Ms. Paige, gave us a pop quiz today in health class. I'm not worried though because I know I passed."

"You better had or I'm gonna fight you," Shannon said pushing up on Jessica. I was a little confused. Was Jessica gay too? Were these two a couple? Before I could ask, Scott came up.

"You ready?"

"Yep. See y'all next week."

They just looked at each other as I walked off. I knew Jessica was gonna try and fish later when she called me tonight.

We walked to the parking lot and got in Scott's car. It wasn't a Lexus but it was a nice Dodge Neon though. Reminded me of a girl car but I didn't tell him that. We drove to my house on Cindy Lane and went in. My mother was still at work and my little sister was probably at her after school tutoring. I didn't have to meet her until six. Thank god. So that just left us two alone. And that's how I wanted it.

"Nice house you have, Desi."

"Thanks. Well let's get to work." We sat down in the living room and we pulled out our books. I wanted to get this math homework knocked out as quickly as possible. I didn't even wanna do it. I would rather be doing Jay right now. Thinking about Jay, I sent him a text to see what he was doing and he said he was at work. I wanted to see him, but he didn't get off until nine. I guess I had to wait. Oh well, at least I had homework to hold me over until then.

We got to number five and I couldn't concentrate anymore. So I started asking Scott questions.

"So, Scott, how old are you?"

"Eighteen. And you?"

"I just turned 18 the other day."

"Oh! Well, happy belated birthday, Desiree. What did you do?"

"My mom cooked as usual. And I had my first time."

"Your first time doing what?"

"Having sex, duh."

"Oh true. If you don't mind me asking, was it your boyfriend?"

"As a matter of fact, it was. Why?"

"At least I know you're not single."

"What's that supposed to mean?"

"It means we can't hangout or anything. I mean you're very beautiful. But I did wanna ask you out and hangout whenever. But you got a man so we can't do anything."

I looked at him out the corner of my eye. He was so damn good-looking it should've been a crime.

"So do you have a girlfriend, Scott?"

"Not at all. I wish you could've been. I've wanted you since I first laid eyes on you."

"Do you want me now?"

"What you mean?"

I didn't even respond. I took our books off our laps and sat them on the floor. I straddled his lap and asked him again as I looked into his hazel eyes. "Do you want me, Scott?"

"What about your boyfriend?"

"I'm not worried about him and neither should you. He can't help me right now but you can."

"Help you with what, Desiree?"

"Help me feed this hunger I have?"

"Are you talking about me fucking you?"

"Hell yes. You've been making my pussy hot since earlier. Hell since the first time I saw you."

"But, Desiree, like I said. What about your boyfriend?"

"Jay? Don't worry about him. What he don't know won't hurt him."

I kissed him and he held back for a second but he eventually got with the program. He grabbed my ass and started squeezing it. I started grinding my pants against his when I started to feel his dick trying to get up through his jeans. He unbuttoned my pants and I stood up so it would be easier for him. My pants dropped to the floor and my purple and black boy shorts were exposed. "Damn. Why you hiding all that ass in them jeans like that, Desiree? Turn around and let me see what you working with."

I did as I was told. I slowly turned all the way around and stopped. I walked back over to him and got back on his lap. We kissed some more and I got hotter. I stood back up, grabbed my pants off the floor, and grabbed his hand. "Get our books."

"Where are we going?"

"To my room."

We got in my room and I locked the door behind us. I pushed him down on the bed and got back on top. I kept dry humping him as I took my shirt off. My titties bounced a little and it seem like it turned him on. I leaned down and kissed him and he ran his hands up and down my back. We were so into it I almost didn't hear my phone ring. I hopped up and grabbed my phone off the table by my bed. It was Jay.

"Hey, Baby," I said, putting a finger over his lips so he wouldn't make any noise.

"What's up with you?"

"Nothing much. Just in here doing homework," I replied. I sat back on the bed as I watched Scott take his shirt off and exposing a toned caramel body that had three tattoos placed nicely on him. I gulped.

"How's work going, boo?"

"Shit, it's cool. I can't wait for it to be over so I can come see my lady."

"Aww, Baby. You're so sweet." Scott was getting back on the bed and was parting my legs. What was he up to? He pulled my underwear off and threw them on the floor. I put his head down between my legs and my eyes got big. Next thing I know, I felt the tip of his tongue brush across my clit. Jay was still on the phone.

"Desiree, did you hear me?"

"Nah, Boo, sorry. I had spaced out for a second."

"I said I gotta get back to work and I will see you tonight. Ok?"

"Ok, Boo."

"I love you."

"Love you, too," I responded. How on earth could I say that and I had another man between my legs? Oh well. There is no turning back now. I hung up the phone with Jay and concentrated on Scott. He was now flicking his tongue back and forth on my pussy. My pussy was getting wetter by the second.

"Oh, Baby," I moaned softly. Now he was kissing and sucking my clit.

"You like that, Baby?"

"Yes."

"Then you're gonna love this." All I felt next was penetration. He had stuck two fingers into my wet pussy. He was simultaneously licking and sticking my pussy. I couldn't take it no more. I grabbed his dreads and shoved his head more between my legs. If it were possible, I would've put his whole damn head inside me. He damn sure knew how to work his tongue. Sheesh.

I pulled him up by his dreads and demanded that he put a condom on. I was ready for that dick. He went into his pocket and pulled out a gold packet. He tore the top off and took the condom out. He put it on and eased it inside of me. I could feel my pussy stretch as he put in each inch. It felt like losing my virginity all over again. Once my pussy adjusted to his penis, it was on. He sped up and I was throwing the pussy at him. He sucked on my neck but I made sure he didn't do it too hard. Didn't need Jay finding out. He moved down to my nipples and started sucking them hard yet gentle at the same time. We started going faster and faster. He came then I came. He kissed me for a few minutes before he got off top.

"Man, that shit was great," he said wiping his forehead.

I got up to go open the window and let some fresh air in. "Yeah, that was good."

"Where did you get that A-1 pussy from?"

"A-1?"

"Yeah. Top of the line. Your pussy is like top shelf liquor," we both laughed at his corny joke. "And might I add, that was some good pussy to eat. I will eat that pussy anytime you want me to."

"That's good to know. I will keep that in mind. That was my first time ever getting my pussy ate. I liked it."

"Shit drop that boyfriend of yours and get with me. It will be plenty more firsts fucking around with me."

I ignored his statement about dumping Jay. I really liked Jay but I liked Scott too. Maybe I could have them both. They just won't know. I got dressed and so did Scott. We finished up our homework and exchanged numbers. Before he left, we kissed again and he ate my pussy until I came. I thought we were gonna have sex again but we didn't. "I'm just gonna leave you with that as a reminder of me, Baby," he said.

With that being said, he grabbed his books and left. I told him I would call him later. I was tired now. I went and took a nap. I almost forgot we were supposed to be going to the movies tonight. I didn't wanna be tired going to the movies or when I met up with Jay.

****

My mom got in from work at 8:30 and I was heading out the door.

"Excuse me. Where are you going, Desiree?"

"Out to the movies with a group of friends."

"How long will you be out?"

"I don't know, mommy. Eleven or twelve I guess."

"Right. Do you have money?"

"Yeah, but I can always have more," I smiled at her as I put my arm around her shoulder. She slid me a twenty, told me to have fun, and to be careful. Typical mother syndrome, I guess. I called Shannon to see where she wanted me to meet them at. She said meet them at Union Station. I hopped on the blue line and rode it all the way to metro center. I got on the red line and rode it to Union Station and went upstairs. I saw Shannon, Jessica, Mario, Matthew, Janay, and Ty standing by the ticket booth. I walked over and spoke to everybody and they spoke back. We purchased our tickets and snacks and went into the theater. As usual, I had to go to the bathroom before the movie started.

I walked to the bathroom and it was empty thankfully. I hated public bathrooms but I hated them even more when it were people in there talking and laughing all loud. I was in the stall when I heard somebody come in and whisper my name. What the hell?

"Desiree are you in here?"

"Who is that? Shannon?"

"Yeah. Are you finished yet? I saved you a seat next to me but you better hurry up. Somebody was eating your popcorn?" she said snickering. I just rolled my eyes because I had a feeling it was her that did it. I came out the stall and went to the sink to wash my hands.

"I been meaning to tell you how good you looked tonight, Desi," Shannon said staring at me in the mirror. I had on a tank top, a pair of shorts and some sandals. What was good about this outfit? I wear this on a regular basis at home.

"Thank you. Don't forget what I told you, Shannon. I'm not a lesbian."

"I remember you telling me that. But you may not be but I am."

"What is that supposed to mean?"

"It means I want you. And I want you bad. I can just taste your pussy on my tongue," she said licking her lips.

"Oh yeah? Then what do I taste like?" I asked flirting with her.

"You taste like strawberries. My favorite fruit. You should let me get a taste."

"Sure why not," I said laughing and moving towards the door. She pushed the door back closed and pulled me into the handicapped bathroom stall. She unbuttoned my shorts and they fell to the floor. She picked me up and put me on her shoulders and went to work with her tongue. I could feel her making circles and figure 8s with her tongue. I held on to the wall that separated the stalls and started humping her face. Just then somebody came in the bathroom. I looked and it was an elderly lady. I tapped Shannon and told her to stop but she didn't. She just kept going. I was struggling to hold in my scream. As soon as the lady left and the door was all the way closed, I let out an orgasmic scream and came all over Shannon's face.

"Damn! Just as I imagined," she said smiling and laughing at me. She grabbed a few paper towels and wet them to clean up our mess from her face and between my legs. I put my shorts back on and we walked back into the movie theater. The movie was already damn near to the middle. Oh well. I thought. I just sat down and watched the movie. Jay had texted me and I told him to meet me there since my mother wasn't expecting me home yet. I texted her and told her I would be home by twelve-thirty at the latest.

After the movie, we all laughed and said what part of the movie was funny to us. I saw Jay pull up so I gave Jessica and Shannon both a hug and walked over to his car. Both Shannon and Jessica were shocked to see me get in the car with Jay and kiss him. We drove off and we headed to his house.

As soon as we got in the house, we started tearing at each other's clothes. We were sucking, biting, and grabbing at each other like we haven't seen each other in forever. We were naked by the time we made it to the couch.

"I want you to do something for me, Baby," Jay said panting.

"What's that?"

"I want you to suck my dick."

"I don't know how to do that but I can try."

"That's cool. Just try, for Daddy."

I took a deep breath and stroked his penis with my hand. I closed my eyes and envisioned everything I saw on the porn videos. I took his manhood in my mouth and started sucking. I grabbed it and stroked it as I rolled my tongue up and down his shaft. My mouth started to get so wet that it sounded like I was slurping his dick.

"Ah, fuck," he yelled.

"What's wrong, Jay? I'm not doing it right? I'm sorry, Baby. I tried my best."

"Don't be sorry, Desi. You're doing great. Are you sure this is your first time?" he asked laughing.

I nodded my head and went back to sucking. He grabbed me by the ponytail and took control of my head movement. He tried to make me deep throat his dick but it wasn't happening. I went for a few more minutes before I stopped and bent over. "I want you to fuck me from behind, Daddy."

He came up behind me and stuck his big dick inside my pussy. Going in slow as he sucked on my neck and nibbled on my ear. Whispering in my ear he said, "This pussy mine and imma take care of it." I could feel his thick shaft getting thicker with each stroke. Going in out and out my pussy with deep thrusts. My pussy getting wetter by the second. I'm soaking up his manhood with my sweet juices. Bent over and throwing it back, making my pussy wetter. Making his dick harder. I can't run away. He's pulling my hair and choking me all at once. Spanking my ass and telling me to be still. I could really get used to getting fucked like this. Oh my god. I can feel my juices run down my leg as my pussy starts to make loud noises. He was fucking me hard and scratching my back. He shoved it in deeper and gripped my waist. He came so hard that he collapsed on my back and just laid there panting. We both were trying to catch our breath and recover.

He rolled off my back and laid down beside me. We start kissing and laughing because we knew we just had great sex. I was sad that I had to go home, but oh well. Even though I'm eighteen, I can't do too much wilding out until school let out. Then it ain't gonna be no stopping me. He drove me home and we made out in the car for about five more minutes. I got in the house a little after midnight but my mother didn't trip. I just went into the bathroom and took a steaming hot shower. I got in the bed and was out before I knew it.

Chapter Five:

Spice It Up

Itold my mother I was gonna spend the day with my sister, Shanice, today. Shanice was my sister on my father's side and she was two years older than me. She was silly like me but crazy as hell. She was not to be fucked with by anybody and she let it be known.

We met up at Pentagon City mall. I wanted to get something nice to wear for Jay tonight, from a store Shanice had told me about. I was just gonna go home, get clothes, and tell my mother I was gonna stay with my sister this weekend. She was actually going with me and chill with Jay's cousin, Mario. So, I had to make sure it was special.

We went into Frederick's of Hollywood lingerie store. It was a nice little boutique in the middle of the mall. I saw all kinds of underwear, bras, corsets, and more. Everything was so jam-packed because the store was so small. I scanned the walls and saw some sexy outfits. I picked up a pretty red lingerie piece. It was made of lace and a peek-a-boo design for the breasts and vagina area. I loved it. I hoped Jay would, too.

Shanice had already paid for hers; a lime green bra and thong set. She even bought some little heels with feathers on them to go with it. I passed on the heels. I walked up to the counter and looked inside the display case. My eyes fell upon a pair of fuzzy metal handcuffs. I decided to buy them along with my outfit. I was beaming inside because I was gonna look great for my Boo. I hope he didn't mind the handcuffs. I saw them use it in a movie I saw and it looked fun. The guy had handcuffed the girl to the bed and made love to her body with his tongue before he dicked her down. That turned me on and I wanted to try it. You know, spice things up a bit.

We went and got something to eat. We sat down in the food court and chit-chatted before going to my house.

"Girl, I don't know why I let you talk me into going with you," Shanice said to me as we sat down with our food.

"Because you are my alibi, duh," I said laughing. "You must plan on giving up some cookies to Mario tonight since you bought that little set."

"I thought it was cute that's why I bought it."

"Mmhmm, yeah, sure you did."

"Okay, okay. So I am gonna give him some nooky. He deserves it."

"How so?"

"Well, we've been kicking it for a while now since your man hooked us up. I just been holding back but he has been so patient."

"I see. All I know is once we go in the room for the night, don't bother us."

"Bitch, please. I'm gonna be too busy getting my pussy ate to be worried about you and your man."

"Likewise."

We finished our food and hopped back on the train to head back to my house. I went in, grabbed an outfit for tomorrow, my scarf, and my personal hygiene stuff. I left my mother a note so she can know where I was. She always tripped when we never told her our whereabouts; grown or not.

We got on the bus and headed to the southeast side of D.C. where my sister lived. Thank god her grandmother, Crystal, wasn't there. I loved her as if she were my own grandma, but those two were always arguing. It was irritating sometimes, sitting there listening to them going back and forth all the time; but it was funny too. You would think they were gonna kill each other. We just chilled around for a bit. I texted Jay the address so he could know where to pick us up from. He said he and Mario would be there at 5:30. It was already 4:30 now. We started to get ready for our men.

Shanice got in the shower first. I sat around and texted Jay, Shannon, and Jessica. Scott texted me but I ignored it. I felt like he was distracting and I didn't want that. Not today. Jessica and Shannon didn't really want anything, except to hangout, but I told them I had plans already. But Jay, mmm. He had recently introduced me to the world of sexting and I was enjoying every minute of it. He sent me a text asking me to send him a picture. I made sure my hair and makeup was good, then I took a selfie and sent it. He texted back with a kissy face and said "go lower."

Oh, he wanna play, do he? I thought to myself. I smiled as I pulled out my right breast and snapped the picture. I knew he would like that because that was his favorite one. I hit send and he replied back quickly. "Go lower" the text read. I knew what he wanted a picture of. I paused and listened for my sister. She was still in the shower. I took my pants and my underwear off. I lay back on some pillows, propped my legs up, and showed my vagina. I sent the picture and smiled. He was such a freak. He texted me back and it read "Ms. Pretty Pussy." I heard the shower cut off and I hurried to put my underwear back on.

"What are you doing?" my sister asked as she came in the room.

"Nothing, Bitch. I was just waiting for your slow ass to finish in the shower." With that being said, I hopped in the shower so I could get ready for Jay.

****

We were having so much fun with Jay and Mario. We had already whooped their asses in spades and scattergories, and they were a little upset. At least, they weren't sore losers. Now, we were just kicking back and watching Friday After Next and hitting some "Mary Jane". I loved this movie but I wanted to do something else. My thoughts, this is good weed, and just being in the presence of Jay, was getting my pussy and my nipples hard. I grabbed Jay by the hand and he just followed without any restraint.

"What's up, Boo?" he asked as soon as I closed the bedroom door.

"I'm tired of sharing you, Baby. I want you all to myself."

"Hey, that's fine with me." He took his shirt off showing his hairy chest and dropped it to the floor. I loved his chest hair. He came towards me and held me in his arms and kissed me. He started to unbutton my pants but I stopped him.

"Uh, uh, uh, mister. Not just yet."

"Why not? What's wrong now?"

"Nothing's wrong, Jay," I said laughing. "I just want you to get out those clothes and I'm gonna run to the bathroom."

"Aight, Baby."

He did as he was told and I slipped out to the bathroom in the hall. I could have used the bathroom in the bedroom but I wanted to spy on my sister and Mario. I tiptoed into the den and saw Mario stroking his dick and playing with my sister's pussy under her skirt. They were so caught up in what they were doing that they didn't even notice my presence; and I'm glad they didn't. It gave me a chance to finally see what Mario was working with.

His dick was so long and black; maybe even a little longer than Jay's. It was just as chocolate as the rest of his body. He reminded me of a snickers bar and looking at him made me hungry. My mind was so much on him and his stroking that I didn't even know that I had started touching myself. I wanted to continue enjoying the show but I had to get back to Jay. But believe me, it wasn't gonna be the last time we would come around one another.

I stood outside the bedroom door and took off my clothes. I opted against going to the bathroom since I was already gone long enough. I didn't want him coming to look for me. I had put the lingerie set on earlier under my clothes so he wouldn't have to wait. I picked up my clothes and walked into the room. Jay was lying back on the bed with his hand behind his head. I dropped my clothes on the floor and stood in front of him.

"My, my, my... Damn, you look good, baby girl," he said standing up in front of me.

"You really like it, Jay?"

"I love it, boo. I love you too."

"Aww… Bae," I said kissing him. "I wanted us to try something new," I said, playing with his chest hair like I always did.

"What?" he asked with raised eyebrows.

"I just wanted to try something new. I hope you don't mind."

"I heard that part," he said laughing. "What did you have in mind?"

"Just sit back and I'll show you."

He got back up on the bed and I went to my bag to grab the handcuffs. I came back twirling them around my finger. He saw them and shook his head no. I nodded my head yes and smiled as I walked towards him. I got on the bed and handcuffed him to the railing.

"Let me take care of you, Daddy," I whispered in his ear. I kissed and nibbled on his ear. I sucked his lobe into my mouth and he moaned softly. I made my way down to his neck, then his chest, leaving a trail of kisses as I headed south. I rubbed my hands across his manhood and slowly took the head into my mouth. I closed my eyes and sucked on the tip before trying my best to suck in every inch of his nine inches. I was getting into my groove when Mario popped in my head. His face was on Jay's face when I opened my eyes. I started sucking faster and harder. I wanted to please Mario. I mean Jay. I got up from between his legs and got on top of him. I loved being on top and in charge.

"Oh shit, Baby," I yelled as soon as I squatted on his dick. I took every inch and it felt good. I rode him for a little while before I removed the cuffs.

He grabbed me around the waist and pulled me off top so he could get a turn. "Now it's my turn to spice things up a bit," he said seductively. He kissed on my neck and my breasts a little. He bit down on my nipples a little harder than usual but it made me moan. He played with my pussy as he continued to kiss on my body. He pulled at the thread where my pussy was slightly covered until it released, exposing it. He dove right in head first. He licked and sucked and fingered my pussy some more. This time he used three fingers. It was feeling so good, better than it usually did. I felt a slight pain and looked down. This nigga was spanking my pussy in between licks. That shit was hot! And it was making me hotter. I moaned loudly and grabbed his head and shoved it back between my legs. If I could, I would chop off his head and take it everywhere with me. Mario popped back in my head and I imagined it being him that was eating my pussy. I don't know what it was about him but I couldn't get him out my mind. Jay was my man but his cousin was gonna get it too.

He moved from between my legs and sat up. He yanked me by my legs and put them up in the air. I thought he was gonna give it to me like that, but boy was I wrong. He handcuffed me to the bed by my ankles. He stuck his dick back in and start pounding away. He got deep inside my pussy and I almost lost my mind. I could feel something stirring deep inside me. I started to clench my pussy muscles. He felt my walls getting tighter on his dick and he fucked me harder and faster. I had come but it wasn't like I normally did. It was more of an explosion. It had gushed out like a wave. I had cum so hard I pushed him out. He dove right back down trying to catch some of my sweet juices as he jerked off. When it was his turn to come, he released my ankles just in time to come all over my chest. It was warm and thick. I made circles in it before I stuck my finger in my mouth.

"You're a bad girl," Jay said kissing me on my forehead.

"I'm your bad girl, Baby," I replied kissing him. We got up to hop in the shower and washed real quick to get each other's body fluids off from each other. We changed the sheets on the bed and laid back down. He held me in his arms like he always did. We heard moans and groans coming from the den. We burst out laughing. It was Mario and Shanice going at it. Her moans were the last things I heard before drifting off to sleep.

Chapter Six:
Caught Up

It had been an exciting weekend. Now it was time to get back to reality. This week was graduation week and I was beyond ecstatic. Jay wanted to come but I didn't know about that. The graduation was Wednesday and I told him I would let him know by tonight. I had to spring it on my mother first. She didn't even know about Jay.

I was in English class when Shannon came in. She had a scowl on her face when she looked at me.

"What the hell is wrong with you, Shannon?"

She just looked at me with such anger in her face. She didn't say anything, just stared at me. She eventually sat down and a few seconds later I received a text from her.

Shannon: You need to leave him alone.

Me: Who?

Shannon: I'm talking about your boyfriend.

Me: Why? Why do I need to leave him?

Shannon: Because I want you.

Me: That was just a one-time thing Shannon. I didn't wanna do anything with you. You did that. It should've never went past that kiss. I love Jay.

Shannon: Jay? Oh that's his name? You surely wasn't thinking about Jay when I had you on my shoulders. You sure wasn't thinking about his ass when I was eating your pussy. And you damn sure wasn't thinking about him when you came all over my face either. But you love him? Smh…you funny.

Shannon was really tripping. No way was I leaving Jay. I loved him. Didn't I? I mean there was that thing I did with Scott but that was a spirit of the moment thing. We haven't done anything in weeks since we had our first encounter. Then there was the thing with Shannon, which should have never happened in the first place.

Me: I'm not leaving my boyfriend, Shannon. I'm sorry if you got caught up in your feelings or whatever the case may be. I love him and I'm gonna be with him. I hope we can still be friends and be cool.

Shannon: So you wanna be friends but not intimate with me? Wanna just act like what happened never happened? Well, it did happen and you liked it.

Me: Yeah, I did like it but I'm still not leaving my dude. Especially not for a female!!! I'm not gay!!! I love dick not pussy!!!

She was starting to piss me off. I felt sorry for her. We were cool so I don't know why she was trying to ruin this over something that was her fault. Hell, she can't blame me for having tasty pussy. Damn.

Shannon: You can keep telling yourself that, but I know better.

Me: Smh. Believe what you want, Shannon. What happened in the past is just that. The past. That's where we're gonna bury it. So are we friends or enemies now?

Shannon: Yeah, you right. We cool. We still gonna be friends. Just think of me when he eating your pussy. I know I do it better anyway.

With that, she stopped texting. At least we were okay now; at least I hope so. I looked up at the teacher and he was still lecturing and writing notes up on the blackboard. Damn, he wrote a lot. I hurried and wrote down everything just in time before the bell rang. I was glad this day was over. It just seemed like today dragged on; like it didn't wanna end.

I was at my locker when I got a text from Jay saying he was outside the school. What was he doing here? I texted back 'okay' and hurried to my locker. I put all my books except my English and history books in my locker. I was trying to rush so fast I didn't even notice Jay come up beside me.

"Hey, Baby," he said, and I jumped.

"Hey, Jay. What's up, boo?"

"Nothing much. What you jumpy for?"

"No reason, Bae. You just scared me a little, that's all. What are you doing here?"

"Dang. Can't a man come pick up his shorty from school and take her home?" he asked, with that smile I loved so much.

"Yes you can. You know what else you can do for me?"

"What's that?"

"For starters, you can give me a kiss. Secondly, you can carry my books for me."

He laughed as he took my books and my book bag. He put his arm around my shoulder and pulled me close to him for a kiss. We had all eyes on us as we kissed right there in the middle of the hallway. I was smiling as I pulled away. I turned and my eyes fell on a disappointed-looking Scott who saw the show. I didn't pay him no mind. I grabbed Jay by the hand and we walked out the school. He opened my door and then put my stuff on the back seat before going around to his side. He was about to pull off when Scott stopped in front of the car. I'm glad Jay was paying attention because he could've hit him.

"What the fuck is this dude doing?" he asked me. He was getting mad,

I could tell. His light complexion was turning pink.

"I don't know, Baby," I said trying to play it off. What the hell was going through Scott's head right now? Don't he know Jay will fuck him up? Jay hopped out the car and went over to Scott.

"Aye, you got a problem, bruh?"

Scott just stood there looking back and forth between me and Jay. Not saying anything. And I wanted it to stay that way.

"What? You can't talk? Are you fucking deaf, Nigga?"

"Not at all. And I can talk. And so can your girl," he responded looking at me. Then Jay looked at me. Oh shit.

"What the hell is that supposed to mean?"

"Ask Desiree." He turned his back on Jay and started to walk away. Jay walked behind him and I got out the car. I grabbed Jay by the hand and told him to get in the car so we could go. He did just that. We got back in the car and he just looked at me.

"What's wrong, Baby?"

"Is there something you wanna tell me, Desiree?"

"No, Boo. Why you ask me that?"

"'Cause he told me to ask you why he said that you can talk. What the fuck that supposed to mean?"

"I don't know, Jay. That dude tripping," I lied. I knew exactly what he was referring to; my moans.

"Yeah, aight. Don't let me find out you doing shit behind my back, Desi."

"I'm not doing anything."

"I believe you. Give me a kiss." I leaned over and gave him a kiss until he released me.

That bamma-ass-nigga Scott ain't shit. Trynna get me caught up. This shit is gonna get messy. I could feel it deep inside me.

We arrived at my house and my mother was in the kitchen. I walked in with Jay behind me. "Ma, can you come here? "I'm in here cooking, Desiree," she said with such sarcasm. So I just grabbed Jay's hand and led him to the kitchen to finally meet my mother.

"Mommy, I wanted you to meet my boyfriend, Jay."

She turned around so fast I thought she had gotten whiplash. "Boyfriend? I didn't even know you liked boys. Didn't know you liked anybody for that matter," she said laughing. I'm glad she was in a good mood. "I'm Denise," she said, shaking his hand.

"It's nice to meet you, ma'am. My name is Jermaine."

Jermaine? How is it that we have been together now for seven months and I never knew his real name? Now it makes me wonder what else he was not sharing with me.

"Well, how old are you? Where do you work? Got any kids?"

Damn. She was bugging. Asking him a million questions all at once. I was a little mad she was asking all these questions but I was curious to hear these answers.

"Well, I'm twenty-three. I work in construction and I have a son who just turned two."

A son? What the hell? He never mentioned a son. Not that I minded, but I would have liked to be informed. Especially if he had baby mama drama.

"Well that's nice. Are you staying for dinner?"

"Sure."

"Okay. Well, y'all run along now. I don't like people out here while I'm cooking. Desiree knows that."

I laughed and kissed her on the cheek. I took Jay into my room. He was watching TV while I worked on my homework. It was an easy assignment. All I had to do for English was to write an essay on a famous person. I decided to do Langston Hughes. I was trying to do my homework, but my mind was still stuck on what Jay told my mother. A son.

"So, Jay. How come I never knew you had a son? How come I never even knew your whole name?"

"Well, Desiree, that answer is simple. You never asked," he said laughing. I laughed too. It wasn't really that serious but I would have liked to know. We started wrestling and making out. My little sister knocked on my door and tried to get in. I'm glad I locked it because her little nosey butt would've busted right up in here. It was time for dinner.

****

Jay and I were now relaxing. My mother said it was cool for him to stay for a while if he wanted to. We were watching Criminal Minds and my phone started going off beside me on my night stand. It was Scott.

Scott: You didn't tell him did you?

Me: There is nothing to tell him Scott.

Scott: So you gonna act like that never happened at your house?

Me: That was a mistake. Why did you do that today? What the hell was that about?

Scott: I just thought he should know about his whore of a girlfriend, that's all.

Me: Whore? I am not a whore. I'm a whore, why? Because I neglect your black ass? Because I don't wanna do shit with you? Nigga please. Fall back.

Scott: Yeah aight. Play like you a good girl but I know the truth.

I didn't even respond back. I just put the phone down and cuddled up with Jay.

"Who was that?"

"Jessica. She was asking me about homework."

"Oh ok. Speaking of homework, I got some homework for you," he said playing with my stomach.

"Oh yeah? What kind of homework?"

He pulled me on top of him and kissed me. He was feeling all over my body and I was feeling all over his. It was starting to heat up. Then my phone rung. I tried to hit the end button but ended up hitting the answer button. I heard yelling and tried to hang it up before he heard it. My crazy ass hit the damn speaker button! All I heard was Scott yelling on the other end.

"You better fucking tell him, Desiree! We had sex and you liked it. You don't want him for real."

Jay heard it and pushed me off of him. "What the hell did he just say?"

"Nothing, Baby," I stammered as I ended the call.

"Nothing? Well, I surely heard something. Who is that, Desi? Is it that bitch ass nigga that I was about to hit earlier? You fucking him, too?"

I just sat there like I didn't hear him. The cat definitely had my tongue. I was trying to think of a lie.

"Hello? I know you fucking heard me."

"Jay, he is tripping, Baby."

"Oh yeah? Then why he say that? Is that who you were texting a lil' while ago?"

"No. I told you that was Shannon."

"No you didn't. You told me you were talking to Jessica."

"That's what I meant, boo," I said laughing a little, trying to play it off. "I was talking to Jessica."

"That's what your mouth say."

"Speaking of my mouth, how 'bout I use it on you?" I asked, tugging at his pants.

"Fuck all that. You ain't putting your mouth nowhere on me until you tell me the truth."

"I am telling you the truth, Jay."

"Give me your phone."

"My phone? What for? Do I ask for your phone?"

"Don't fucking play with me, Desiree. I will fuck you up. Because I got respect for your moms, I won't fuck you up in this house. Now give me your fucking phone," he said through clenched teeth.

I knew he wasn't playing. He hit me before with no problem. There was one doubt in my mind that he would do it again. Or do something worse. I obliged and gave him the phone. He opened up my messages and stood next to me.

"You surely been texting a lot today while you were supposed to be in class," he said referring to Shannon's texts. He opened those back up and scrolled. His eyes got wide and he shook his head. He didn't say anything but I knew he was hurt. I could see it written all over his face. "So you let a girl eat your pussy at the movies, huh? That's wild. And then you had sex with me right after? You have no morals, do you?" he asked, letting out a sarcastic chuckle. He exited out of the texts with Shannon and scrolled back up. "I thought you said you were texting Jessica this time of night?"

"I was texting Jessica, Jay."

"Oh ok. Well, how come I don't see her name? But I do see Scott's name as the last person you were texting." He got quiet again and scrolled through those messages. He didn't even say anything after he closed the messages. He just grabbed his phone and keys off the bed and brushed past me.

"Jay, where are you going?" I asked pulling on his arm. He yanked away from me and walked out the room then out the front door. I trailed behind him outside, only wearing boy shorts, a t-shirt, and ankle socks. I got outside and grabbed him again but he pushed me away.

"Jay, please. I'm sorry baby. I didn't mean to do it."

"You sorry for what? For being a slut? For having me look like a damn fool? Or are you just sorry you got caught? Which is it?"

"I'm sorry for hurting you, Baby."

"Bitch please. You weren't worried about hurting me when you opened your legs not once, but twice, for two other people," he said turning his back on me and going to his car. I caught up to him right before he got in the car. I pulled him again. He backhanded me and threw me against the car with his hand wrapped around my throat. He was choking me so hard I couldn't breathe.

"Look you little whore, just face it. You got caught and that's cool. If that's what you wanna do then do it. I knew I should've never fucked with your ass. All y'all virgins do the same thing. Like what I give you wasn't enough. Well cool. Go get it from every Tom, Dick, and Harry that you want. This dick ain't never coming back this way. Lose my fucking number while you at it."

He let go of my neck and pushed me away from his car. He got in the car and started it up while I gasped for air. When I got back up, all I saw was tailights turning the corner. I was lonely now. Not only was Jay gone but he took with him a piece of my heart and left me with a lot of guilt for what I had done. Now what was I gonna do?

Chapter Seven:
Need To Release

This past week has been ridiculous. I lost Jay, Shannon been trying to comfort me in her own way, and Scott just keeps texting me. I know I was wrong for what I did to Jay but it was a mistake. Why couldn't he understand that? I didn't mean to hurt him. I had just got caught up in the moment with Shannon and Scott. I missed Jay. He wasn't answering my calls or my messages. Eventually, I got added to the block list. I guess we were really over.

Well, now that school was over for me, I needed to find some attention for my body. Since Jay wasn't available, who could I run to now for satisfaction? I was so lost. Maybe a job would take my mind off of Jay. I can make money and keep busy and over time push him to the back of my mind. I looked in the newspaper and saw that they were hiring at a pizza place not far from my old neighborhood. They were doing one-on-one interviews all day today. I decided to go and apply. What could it hurt? The worst they can say is no.

I went into my closet to look for interview clothes. I didn't really have anything for that occasion but I'm sure I could figure something out. I chose a belted black dress that came down to my knees and some heels. I never wore them but, surprisingly, I could walk in them. I looked myself over in the mirror and I looked good. I should wear heels more often. I liked how good they made my legs and my ass look. I asked my mother for the car keys, grabbed a couple of resumes and left.

I got to the restaurant and was surprised to see Jessica there.

"What are you doing here?"

"The same reason you're here, crazy lady," she said and we laughed. "I need a job."

"True shit."

We sat there talking until a girl came out and called Jessica's name. I wished her luck as she headed into the office. The girl was really cute. What the hell was I talking about? Ever since Jay broke up with me the other day, I have been thinking that both men and women were attractive. I needed help.

Jessica came out fifteen minutes later, smiling from ear to ear. It didn't take a rocket scientist to know that she got the job. "Congratulations," I said to her as she approached me.

"Thank you, girl. You want me to wait for you?"

"Naw, I'm good. After I finish, imma head home. What you doing later?"

"Not sure yet. Just call me."

"Okay," I said as I gave her a hug. As soon as I sat back down, they called my name. Here goes nothing. I walked into the office to see a brown skinned man that looked to be in his forties or fifties sitting behind the desk. The girl left, leaving us alone.

"Well, Ms. Logan. I'm John and I will be interviewing you today. Tell me a little about yourself."

"Well, I'm eighteen years old and I just graduated from high school. I have worked before but it wasn't in food service. It was childcare. I am a great worker and I work hard."

"That's what I like to hear. I see you applied for a cashier position. You think you can handle it when we get those rushes on the weekend?"

"If I can handle rowdy kids for eight hours a day then being a cashier will be like a walk in the park."

"That's what I like to hear. You can start tomorrow. You can wear your own jeans and comfortable shoes. When you come in tomorrow, you will get a uniform shirt. Any questions?"

"Just one. What time should I be here?"

"Be here at ten."

"Ok. No problem."

We stood up at the same time. He came around the desk and shook my hand. He was holding on to it longer than he was supposed to, so I did the honors of letting go of his. I thanked him and turned to walk to the door. He was right on my heels trying to beat me to the door. He must have gotten a look at my ass. Silly rabbit. He better calm down before he hurt himself. His ass would end up having a heart attack fucking with me. I'm just saying. He wasn't bad looking but he was the farthest thing from my mind. I got in the car and rushed home to tell my mother the good news.

I got there and my sister was there. "Where's mommy at?"

"In her skin," she said, laughing.

"Look, you little unwanted species, where is ma?"

"If youhad looked, you would've known she was in the room, stupid." I just shook my head as I walked off. Why couldn't I have been an only child? I thought to myself. I went into my mother's room and she was in there watching her soaps. I stood there and waited for it to go on commercial before I told her the good news.

"Ma, guess what?"

"You're moving out?"

"Are you crazy?" I asked her laughing. "No seriously?"

"I am serious."

"Anyway, I got a job."

"That's good. Where at?"

"A pizza place around where we used to live at. It's called Pizza Palace. I start tomorrow."

"I'm happy for you, Desiree. Now move before you make me miss something."

I shook my head and smiled. My mother loved these shows for some reason.

I went into my room and got on Facebook to share my news with the world. I was so excited I couldn't contain myself. That's just what I needed. I grabbed my phone when I heard the notification chime. It was Scott texting me.

Scott: Hey Desiree, what you up to?

Me: What the fuck you want, Scott?

Scott: Damn, why the hostility? I just wanted to know if you wanted to kick it with me.

Me: What are you up to?

Scott: Nothing. I know I fucked up your relationship by saying something and I wanted to make it up to you. I'm sure you miss seeing me.

He was right I did miss hanging out with him. Other than that time we had sex, we had fun hanging out at each other's houses. I decided to go chill with him for a bit.

Me: What are we gonna do?

Scott: Well, we can watch a movie. I know how much you love Michael Myers.

Me: LOL. You're right about that. Let me change my clothes and I will be over there.

Scott: Ok. See you soon.

I changed into some yoga pants, a t-shirt, and my new balance. I looked good even on my chill swag. Maybe I could get some new bait on my line before the day was over. I grabbed my cell phone and my keys before leaving.. Thankfully Scott only lived three blocks from me. The hounds were out today. One guy was even bold enough to grab my hand, trying to get my attention. I snatched away and kept walking. I got on the phone so they could stop bothering me. I called Jessica.

"Hey girl," she said as soon as she picked up. "How did your interview go?"

"It went good. I got the job."

"Oh yeah. That's what's up. It's gonna be fun working together."

"Yeah, I know. I can't wait. Did you decide what you were doing tonight?"

"Not doing nothing. You wanna come over? My dad won't mind."

"Sure. I'll be over later. I'm about to go over Scott's house and chill."

"Ooh, Scott. What's going on between you two?"

"It's not even like that, honey," I said laughing. "I just wanna be around some male company. Since Jay and I broke up, I been kind of bored just seeing your ass all the time."

"Bitch please. You love me," she said, laughing and making kissing noises into the phone.

"Yeah, that's true. But I'm here now so I will hit you up when I'm on my way."

"Have fun. But not too much," she said, laughing. I hung up and shook my head. She was a mess but I loved her crazy butt.

I walked up on Scott's porch and before I could knock on the door, he opened it.

"Hey, Baby," he said leaning in, trying to kiss me.

"Uh, uh, dude," I said mushing his face back. "I'm not your baby and don't be trying to kiss me. I was serious about what I said."

"Sticking to your guns, I see. I just thought you might have changed your mind. You can't blame a guy for trying."

"Hell yeah! So now, where's the movie at?"

"Right in the living room."

"Then let's go."

We went into the living room and he had a stack of every Halloween movie stacked on the table. I went to sit down and he sat down beside me. Too damn close for comfort if you ask me. I scooted over and so did he. This was gonna get on my nerves. I already knew it.

"Can you chill, Scott?"

"I'm not doing anything. How you gonna get mad because I wanna be next to your fine ass?"

"Negro, please. Don't think I forgot about what you did."

"I told you I was sorry. Let me make it up to you."

"How?"

"I'm not gonna tell you. I wanna show you."

"I think I'm gonna pass then."

"True."

He stopped talking and we just continued to watch Halloween. I was getting thirsty so I excused myself and went to get something to drink. I was rummaging through the fridge when Scott came up behind me.

"What the hell are you doing?" I asked him when I felt him brush up against me.

"Just enjoying the view," he replied licking his lips.

I stood up and rolled my eyes at him. I grabbed an orange soda out the fridge before closing it. I popped the can open and took a big gulp. I was looking right at him and I could see his dick jump in his pants. I walked away and grabbed a banana off the counter as I headed back to the living room. He followed.

We got back in the living room and sat down. I peeled the banana peel back and stuck half the banana down my throat before softly biting it. I could see Scott out the corner of my eye. He was sitting there like an idiot with his mouth open, staring at me. I laughed on the inside because his face was priceless.

"Can I rub your feet?"

"Can you what?"

"Can I rub your feet?"

"Um, why?"

"Because you look like you got pretty feet. They might stink a little but they probably pretty as hell," he said laughing.

I playfully punched him in the arm before putting my feet across his lap. I put the banana peel down and patiently waited. He took my shoes off and started massaging my feet. This was cool. I turned my attention back to the movie while he continued. I was all into the movie.

I felt something warm and wet on my feet. I looked and he was running his tongue across my toes. His tongue was all warm and wet. It was feeling good. He was rolling his tongue all over my foot, through the cracks between my toes, sucking on each toe, one by one. I started to moan low and he noticed. He massaged my foot and sucked on my toes some more. He rolled my pants leg up and kissed up my calf. I started shifting in my seat. He pulled me down on the sofa and got on top of me. He started kissing on my neck and playing under my shirt.

"Scott, no," I said moaning.

"No what?"

"I don't wanna do anything. Stop. You're making me horny."

"That's good. You made me horny as soon as I saw you walk up with those pants on."

He began to dry hump me. I could feel his penis get hard. My pussy started to awaken. It felt like his dick was about to bust out his pants. I pushed him off me and stood up. "I'm leaving, Scott."

"Why? I thought you were enjoying yourself?"

"I was, until you started jumping my bones."

"I'm sorry. Let's just finish watching TV."

"Naw, I'm good, Scott. We can finish this another time. When I'm in the mood. Okay?"

"That's cool. I will see you later."

"Yeah," I said. I gave him a soft kiss on the cheek before I put my shoes and socks back on and left. That turned me on so much. I had to get out of there before I had sex with him again. Not that I wouldn't mind it, I just wasn't ready. Now, I'm all hot and bothered and needed to find some sexual relief.

****

I got to Jessica's house and told her everything that happened at Scott's house. She found it hilarious. It did seem funny when it was said out loud. My mind was still on it though. When he was playing with my toes, I had pre-came in my panties. I wiggled my toes just thinking about it.

"You have the most fun times when I'm not around," Jessica said laughing.

"If you say so. What time will your dad be home?"

"I don't know. Why?"

"Because I wanted to smoke before he got here."

"Oh okay. Well, we can go on the back porch. He doesn't mind but we can't smoke in the house. Come on," she said leading me through the kitchen. I lit my blunt before I even got out the door. I took a deep pull and held it for a few seconds before exhaling. In with the good shit and out with the bullshit. I passed the joint to Jessica who pulled it as hard as I did.

"So what you end up doing after you left the interview, Jess?"

"I went to the mall. I met this guy named Danny."

"Finally. I thought you would never meet anybody," I said jokingly.

"Whatever, bitch. He wanted to see me for a little while tonight but I told him no because you were coming over."

"Why the hell would you do that? He wanted to take you out?"

"No, crazy ass. He just wanted to see me for a little bit when he got off work."

"Well, what time does he get off?"

"I think he said eleven."

"Well call him and tell him he can stop by. I don't mind."

"You sure?" she asked as she hastily pulled her phone out.

"You better do it before I do it," I said laughing. She walked off and called him while I continued to hit the weed. She came back a few minutes later, gleaming, saying he was gonna stop by.

"That's cool. Tell him to send you a picture so I can see how he look."

"Okay, hold on." She had texted him. He sent a picture back fairly quick. She showed me the picture and I must admit, he was really cute. He looked like he was mixed or something. I gave her my approval and we went back in the house.

We went into Jessica's room and watched a Martin marathon that was on. The evening was slowly coming to an end and it was almost 10:30 at night.

"Time for you to get ready for your date, Jess."

"Bitch. It's not a date. We just gonna kick it for a bit in the car. We might ride around to the park. You know I have nosey ass neighbors."

"That you do," I said laughing. "So what are you going to wear?"

"Well, let's see. Clothes. I'm gonna keep on what I have on. I will just take a shower when I get back in."

"I guess. Well, I'm about to take a shower now, if you don't mind." I grabbed a towel and washcloth off her shelf then grabbed my bag. When I was going out the room, her dad was on the other side of the door. "Hey, Mr. Cooper."

"Hey, Desiree. Girl, do you ever stay home?" he asked laughing.

"Yeah, whenever your daughter kicks me out."

"Which never happens," Jessica yelled down the hall when I walked away. I heard them talking as I headed into the bathroom. I know it was wrong, but Jessica's dad was attractive in some type of way.

Mr. Cooper was divorced and single. He had black hair with a little gray mixed in. He looked good to be in his early 50s, honestly. He was a little big but his height made him appear like an average middle-aged man. I had better watch it around him. Better yet, he better watch himself around me. I was in the shower when I heard a knock on the door. "Who is it?"

"It's Jessica. Can I come in?"

"It's your house."

"You always being fucking smart," she said coming in and closing the door. "So Danny said he was five minutes away. I don't know how long I'm gonna be out so you don't have to wait up for me."

"Oh, yes I do. I wanna here all the juicy details."

"There won't be any."

"That's what your mouth say."

"I'm serious. I'll be back shortly," she said, as she reached into the shower and gave me a quick hug and a kiss on my cheek.

"Be careful. Text me his tag number just in case. You know how we do."

"Okay. See you later."

She left the bathroom and I showered for a few more minutes before getting out. I wrapped the short towel around me and grabbed my belongings and went into the room. I went into Jessica's room and peeked out the window, just in time to see Jessica and Danny pull off. I grabbed the baby oil gel so I could moisturize my skin. My phone buzzed as soon as I put the clear liquid in the palm of my hand. Ain't this a bitch? I looked at the text and it was the license plate number. Then my phone buzzed again before I could put it back down. This time it was Shanice telling me she broke up with Mario. That really wasn't news. I figured that was coming. She said she was gonna break up with him anyway because she started talking back to her ex. All that meant was Mario was now available on the chopping block. I texted her back 'okay' and put my phone back on the bed.

I was finally able to oil up my legs. I propped my leg up on the bed so I could put it all over my foot and everything. Then I did the other leg. As soon as I put that leg up on the bed, Mr. Cooper came in the room. He just stood there.

"Hey, Mr. Cooper. What's up?" I asked like I wasn't sitting there fully naked.

"Uh. Um," he said stumbling over his words. "Um, where is Jessica?"

"She went out with a friend for a little while."

"Oh ok. Well, bye," he said and quickly exited the room.

I laughed because I knew that had caught him off guard. No way was he expecting to see me like that. Oh well. He got a chance to see me naked. It didn't bother me at all. I don't know why on earth it bothered him. I finished oiling up my body then threw on a night shirt. I decided to read for a little bit.

I eventually looked at the clock and it was a little after 1. Jessica still wasn't back yet. I texted her to know if she was okay and she texted back a thumbs up emoji. Well, I guess I had to chill for a little bit longer than planned. I wanted a snack. I needed something to take my mind off being alone and, even after taking a shower, my hormones were still raging. I thought reading would take my mind off it but it didn't. I will probably watch some porn.

I walked to the kitchen and Jessica's dad was there. He was sitting at the table reading a newspaper and he didn't even realize I was there.

"What are you reading, Mr. Cooper?" I asked, startling him.

"Just a few stories about this crazy world we live in. Look, I wanna excuse myself for walking in on you earlier."

"It's cool. It was a mistake."

"Exactly."

I reached in the fridge and grabbed a handful of Jessica's strawberries out the container. I put them in a foam bowl and sprayed whipped cream on top of them. I excused myself and sashayed back to Jessica's room. I knew he was watching me walk away and I laughed inside.

I got to the bedroom and closed the door. I searched through the channels until I turned on Cinemax. Now this is what I need. They were airing a flick of sexual fantasies. The woman was blindfolded and the guy was skillfully taking his time with her body. That's what I need. That's what I had with Jay. I wanted that again with somebody else. I continued to watch and eat the strawberries. When they were gone, I sat the bowl aside and focused on the screen. My eyes were glued to the TV. I didn't wanna miss a beat. I heard a knock at the door and I quickly changed the channel.

"Hey, I'm going to bed, Desiree. Holler if you need anything," Mr. Cooper said from the other side of the door.

"Okay. Good night, Mr. Cooper." I heard him drag his feet across the floor. Once I heard his door close, I turned the movie back on. The guy was now pouring hot wax over the woman's torso. She was moaning loudly, but that shit looked like it burned. It did look fun though. He then laid her across the back of a chaise and pulled out a paddle. He starting spanking her with it. Her ass jiggled with each slap. Her ass cheeks were turning red and I was getting turned on. I started touching my breasts and my vagina, as I watched the two of them go at it. My hands so weren't doing the job. I went to my backpack and pulled out my friend. I called him Kong. He was long, black and strong just like King Kong the gorilla. He has been helping me out when I couldn't get a partner to help me release my frustrations. I locked the door then laid up on the bed. I propped my legs up and inserted Kong inside my pussy. I was already wet which was good. I didn't have to waste any time getting her ready. I closed my eyes and imagined that the guy on the screen was doing everything to me. I pushed my dildo deep inside me and pulled him back out repeatedly. It was feeling good, but I needed a little help. It was almost two and Jessica still wasn't back. I texted her to see how long she would be and she said another hour. Good answer.

I tiptoed out the room with Kong in my hand. I listened at Mr. Cooper's door. I didn't hear nothing but light snoring. I twisted the lock and the door opened. I could see his silhouette with the help of the little light that came through the window. He only had on boxer briefs. This was gonna be easy.

I closed the door behind me as I stepped into the room. I got up on the bed gently. I didn't want to wake him. I made sure he was still asleep before I reached inside his boxers. I pulled out his limp dick and massaged it. I sucked on Kong as I stroked Mr. Cooper's penis to life. He started to stir and I paused. When he stopped, I continued. I guess it was meant for me to suck his dick because it woke up a few moments later. I took the toy out of my mouth and put it inside my pussy. I wrapped my lips around the head of his penis and continued to stroke it.

He woke up out of his sleep and turned on his bedside lamp. I didn't even stop. I looked up at him and he looked back at me as I sucked on his dick. "What are you doing?" he asked in a hushed tone.

"I was bored and horny," I said, as I continued to stroke his dick. He just looked at me in amazement. Not another word was said. He laid back on his elbows and watched me work. He threw his head back as I tried to put it all in my mouth. I gagged a little. His penis was more fatter than anything. I have never seen anything like it before. He pulled me up and laid me on my back. He got up and locked the door. He came back to the bed and put my legs over his shoulder while I was still laying down. He ate my pussy good, too. He used his fingers and his tongue. His tongue felt like a little dick as it penetrated my pussy. I came a little then moved him out the way. I wanted to get on top but he wasn't having it. He rolled me onto my stomach and had me arch my back. He noticed Kong on the bed when it touched his leg. "What is this?" he asked.

"Oh that's my friend, Kong. I was using him before and after I came in here."

"I see. Do you still wanna use him?"

"Not if I can have you inside me instead."

"Have you ever had double penetration before?"

"No."

"Well, you will now."

He spread my pussy lips open and stuck Kong inside of me. Oh shit. He was doing a better job than I was. I felt his tongue on my ass cheeks and I moaned. His warm tongue felt good. He left the dildo inside of my pussy and used his hands to stretch my ass cheeks open. He licked my ass and stuck his tongue all in my asshole. Damn. Jay had never done that before and I wished like hell he had.

I felt him stick a finger in my asshole and I jerked. "Calm down. I'll be gentle." I listened and relaxed. He penetrated my ass with his long index finger as he started using Kong in my pussy again. He pulled Kong out after a few strokes and stuck his own dick inside me. He fucked my pussy with his dick and my ass with his finger at the same damn time. I yelped when I felt the head of my dildo in my hole.

"Ouch that hurts."

"That's only because you're thinking about it. Focus your mind on this good dick that's taking care of your pussy. I won't hurt you."

He went back to fucking me and stuck the toy back in my ass. The pain eventually subsided and I started moaning. This double penetration was bomb. Made me wonder how it would feel if another man was inside of me instead of the toy. He continued the double penetration until I had come. He took the toy out my ass and grabbed me by the hips. He fucked me faster and when he came, he pushed his dick deep inside me. It felt like he was in my stomach. I felt his sperm release all inside of me. That was fun.

He gave me a good night kiss on the lips and slipped me his number before I left the room. I took a quick shower to hide the evidence. I went back and laid down. I heard the front door open and close. It was Jessica. I turned over and created the illusion that I was asleep. She came in the room and called my name. I guess she figured I was asleep since I didn't respond. She grabbed some clothes and went into the bathroom to shower. I knew she was gonna tell me all about it in the morning. Me, however, I wasn't gonna tell her anything that happened tonight.

I put my hands down between my legs. I had a tingly feeling. Not a bad one. A great one. I was going to sleep with a smile on my face and my pussy satisfied.

Chapter Eight:

Want That Old Thing Back

It was my first day at Pizza Palace and it was hectic. People were ordering food inside and over the phone. Why couldn't their lazy asses just cook for Christ sakes? This shit was ridiculous. Jessica was busy making pizza after pizza and I was taking all the orders. Luckily, we worked fast because if we hadn't, it would be a wreck.

It was six o'clock and officially time for my break. I clocked out and went to go sit in Jessica's car. I had four text messages. One from my mom, one from Shannon, one from Scott, and lastly Jay. What was Jay doing texting me? Maybe it was a mistake. I opened the message and all it said was 'can we talk?' I texted back "yes." Maybe it wasn't a mistake. My phone beeped. It was him again.

Jay: Cool. Where are you? Are you home?

Me: no, I'm at work.

Jay: work? You got a job?

Me: yes, I did. I work at Pizza Palace in NE. I get off at 11.

Jay: I know just where that is. Is it okay if I pick you up?

Me: sure.

Jay: See you later.

What kind of game was he playing? He broke up with me and I honestly was not expecting him to ever contact me anymore. It would be nice to see him though. I read my other messages. Shannon didn't want anything but for us to hangout again. The same with Scott. My mom just wanted to know what time I got off. When my break was over, I went back inside and saw that it had calmed down tremendously, which was cool. I told Jessica that Jay wanted to talk to me and she shook her head.

"What's all that for?"

"Because, Desiree, what does he want? He done knocked you upside your head for that shit Scott pulled and you still wanna see him. Both of y'all asses are crazy if you ask me."

"I know, but I love him, Jess. It won't hurt just to hear what he has to say."

"If you say so," she responded, ending the conversation.

We continued through our shift, just joking around like we did until it was time to go. When we got outside, Jay was outside waiting on me. I told Jessica I would talk to her tomorrow if not tonight. We were both off tomorrow, so we would probably kickback and chill. I got in the car and he pulled off after I buckled my seat belt. We drove all the way to the park without speaking a word. Just the radio station was on, playing slow jams. This was new. He usually only played rap music in his car.

"So what's been up with you, shorty?" he asked me.

"Nothing much. Just trying to maintain. Ever since you broke up with me, I've had a lot of time on my hands," I said sarcastically. "How about yourself?"

"Shit just been working and chilling. I have been thinking about you though. About us."

"Us? What us, Jay?"

"Me and you, babe. I miss you. I want us to try this again. What you think?"

"Why? I mean, don't get me wrong, I missed you too."

"I just said because I missed you. I miss seeing you and I been missing your body."

"Oh, so that's what this is about? You need some pussy? Why didn't you just ask?"

"I mean, hell yeah! I need some. What man doesn't? I didn't wanna just come right out and ask you something like that."

"Just ask. Asking questions never hurt anyone."

"Well, Desi, can we go somewhere and have sex? I haven't had any since we broke up and I'm backed up."

"Why would we go somewhere? We can do it right here. You got a condom?"

"Yeah, but we gonna do it right here?"

"Yep. Right in the backseat," I said climbing over the seat. I took my pants off and sat there waiting.

"What if we get caught?"

"Look, if you scared say you scared. You can either get the pussy now or you can wait for somebody else."

"Shit, make some room."

He climbed over the seat into the backseat with me. He bent me over and pulled his dick out through the hole in his jeans. He pulled my pants down to my knees and was about to insert his penis until I stopped him. "Put the damn condom on, Jay. I'm not playing with you."

He exhaled loudly but he put one on. I could tell he was mad but I didn't really give a damn. He could've been fucking some dirty bitch raw but he won't fuck me like that. Not anymore. He put his dick in and we fucked for all of twenty minutes. When we both came, he pulled out and I pulled my pants back up.

"Damn, baby. What if I wanted to go again?"

"Oh well, you short, homie. I'm ready to go home."

"So it's like that? Did you think about what I said?"

"I will think about it."

"When will I have an answer back?"

"Later this week. Maybe Tuesday or Wednesday at the latest."

"Aight," he said shaking his head. We got back in our seats and he drove off. "You hungry? We can stop somewhere and grab something to eat."

"Naw, I just wanna go home."

"Okay." He said nothing else. He just drove me home. We pulled up at my building and I hopped out and closed the door. As I walked in the building, Jessica called. I answered.

"Bitch, what happened?" she yelled into the phone.

"If you don't calm down, broad," I responded laughing. "He just asked if we could try it again. And we had a quickie."

"You nasty little girl," she said laughing. "Well what did you tell him?"

"That I would let him know later in the week."

"Come on, D. You're not actually considering being with him again are you? I mean what does he actually do that makes you happy?"

"He sweet when he wants to be. He texts me all the time to check on me. And the sex is great. And I love him."

"You love him, huh? I think that's a bunch of bull but you're my girl, so I gotta act happy for you."

"And I thank you for that, madam. But I'm about to hop in the shower and go to bed. You're off tomorrow right?"

"I was, but John asked me to work tomorrow."

"Oh okay. Well, I guess I'm gonna just lay around the house tomorrow and watch LMN."

"Oh gosh. That's for miserable people. Just call one of your boyfriends. Who you wanna chill with? Scott or Jay?" she said, laughing hard.

"Neither," I responded sternly. I didn't find that shit funny. I hung up on her and got ready for my shower. I needed a nice hot steamy shower. I had to gather my thoughts. Did I really wanna be back with Jay? I did love him but I loved his sex more. Or did I love him more? Not really sure.

I got out the shower and grabbed my phone. Jay had texted me a kissy face emoji and I smiled. I texted back 'yes' to him. He responded back with a cheesy face. I put on my pjs and laid down for the night. I was beat.

It was 3 a.m. when my phone had rang. I didn't know who it was but I answered anyway.

"Hello?" I said groggily into the microphone.

"Hey, Desiree. What's up?" It was a guy.

"I'm good. Who is this?"

"Damn, you don't know my voice by now?" he said, laughing.

"Look, I don't have time for this shit. I'm bout to hang up."

"Chill. Don't hang up. It's me, Mario."

Mario? What the hell did he want? Better question is how did he get my number in the first place? "Um, hi, Mario. Not that I don't fucks with you like that but how did you get my number? Better yet, what in your right mind possessed you to call my phone at some damn three in the morning, my nigga?"

"I took it out of Jay's phone one day. I hope you don't mind me calling you. But I knew at this time of night, I could catch you by yourself."

"Nigga. These are booty call hours. I shouldn't have even answered it."

"Well, since you did answer my call can I come get some booty?" he asked laughing into the phone.

"Cute. Real cute. What do you want, Mario? I'm tired."

"I wanted to know if you were busy tomorrow. I needed your help with something."

"Which is what?"

"Help me go shoe shopping."

"You joking right? Why you didn't ask Shanice to go with you or one of them hoes that be on your dick?"

"Because if you like my cousin, I know you got good taste," he laughed. I laughed with him because that was a little true.

"Yeah, I'll go. I guess. What time are picking me up?"

"Be ready at 8."

"8? In the morning?"

"Yeah. I wanna make sure you have breakfast ready for daddy." I hung the phone up in his ear. He called back and I let it go to voicemail. He texted 'be rdy @ 12.' I didn't respond. I turned over and went back to sleep. That nigga was crazy.

****

Nymphopervtress

My alarm went off at 10:30. I got up and started getting ready. I chose to wear a maxi dress and flip flops. I was gonna go and get my feet done while we were at the mall. I unwrapped my hair and brushed it. I had it in pin curls so it didn't take long to take out then style. I ate me a breakfast sandwich and turned on Lifetime. I texted him and told him I was ready. He texted back "okay" and that he would be there shortly.

I was watching this movie called 'If Someone Had Known' and it was crazy. The guy was beating his wife. It made me sad to watch these kinds of movies but they were interesting to watch. Is this what love was? Did love actually hurt? I didn't know. I have only been loved by one person and that was Jay. He hit me those couple of times but I knew that he only did that because he had gotten upset. If I stopped doing things to make him mad then he wouldn't hit me. I will test that theory later this week.

Mario had called me and told me he was outside. I grabbed my phone and keys and left. He was sitting in his black Cadillac Escalade truck waiting for me. I climbed up in the truck and closed the door.

"You're looking good, Desiree."

"Thank you."

"So what mall are we going to?"

"I guess we can hit Forestville Mall first."

"Good. I need to go get my nails and my feet done."

"Damn, both? That's gonna take like five hours."

"Nigga, please. One hour tops."

"That's cool I guess."

"You act like you have to sit there. I didn't ask you to babysit me."

"True. Well I won't."

"Good." We drove off and headed to the mall. The nail salon wasn't packed yet. I guess everybody was still at church or at home making Sunday dinner. I walked in and wrote down my name and what I wanted. A few minutes later, the guy came back and took me to a seat for my pedicure. Mario followed behind me. "I'm good from here, dad," I said to him as I sat down.

"Dad, huh? Oh you real funny. You're a regular old Mo'nique."

"That's a little overboard but I guess."

"Here you go," he said handing me some money.

"I got money."

"I know you do but this is for me waking you up last night. The least I can do is pay for you to get pampered since you came out with me."

"Good point," I said, grabbing the cash out his hand.

"I'm gonna wait for you over there. I just gotta make some calls."

"You don't have to wait for me. I told you."

"What I say?"

"Cool. Whatever," I responded and he walked off. I was in heaven as the guy massaged my feet before tending to it. It reminded me of when Scott had done it. I wish it was Scott doing it now. His tongue felt so good that day. Once the guy finished, he took me to a nail table to do my nails. He was done with my nails in twenty minutes. I looked at the time. I was only there for 45 minutes. I got up and walked over to Mario. "All finished," I said.

"It took you long enough. Let me see." I held up my hand and stuck out my foot so he could see. "Looks good. I could've done better though."

"Not on me, slim," I said laughing. I paid the guy and we left. I tried to give Mario the change but he declined. He didn't have to tell me twice. We walked into Foot Locker. He said he wanted the new Jordans that had come out that weekend. He showed them to me.

"You like these?" he asked pointing to some red, white, and silver Jordans. "These are the Air Jordan 7 Retro. These are the Hares."

"They look cute."

"You think so? Would you wear them?"

"Yeah." He waved the shoe salesman over and told him to bring back those shoes in both of our sizes. "Are you crazy, Mario?"

"What? You said you liked them. So I'm gonna buy them for you. Is that okay?"

"Yeah, sure." I wasn't gonna complain. Let him buy them. Shit Jay never bought me Jordans but he did buy me that necklace that I still wear around my neck. I wonder if he noticed that the other night. Whether he did or not, now was not the time to be thinking about him. I was focused on Mario. He was already attractive. His money enhanced that to the extreme. We did a little window shopping for a little bit. He kept trying to buy me stuff but I declined. We left the mall and got in the truck.

"When was the last time you talked to Jay?" he asked out the blue.

"I haven't heard from Jay since we broke up," I lied.

"So does that mean we can kick it?"

"Yeah. We friends, right?"

"Right." Instead of taking me home, we drove to his house in Largo. He had a nice two-level townhouse. He showed me around before we settled in what he called his 'movie room'. He had a couple of movie theater seats and a projector and screen in there. Made me wonder how much money he really had. Also, what the hell did he even do for a living?

"So what do you do for a living?"

"I'm a hustler, baby," was all he said. No further questions.

We sat down and he hit play. The screen came down from the ceiling and the movie started. It was Straight Outta Compton. I had already seen it but this was one of those movies that I could watch more than once. We were sitting there watching the movie and he put his arm around me. I didn't move or anything. I didn't see a problem with it. I had felt my phone vibrate in my pocket and I took it out. It was Jay calling. I stopped it from vibrating and cut my phone completely off. I was having fun and I didn't want any distractions; especially Jay. He would kill us if he found out.

I leaned over and kissed Mario on the cheek. "What was that for?"

"I don't know. Just thanking you for a good afternoon."

"Anytime."

We finished watching the movie and he cooked a little something for us to eat. We were sitting across from each other at the table when he looked at me. "I really enjoyed spending time with you today. And if it's definitely over with you and Jay, I would love for us to kick it some more. I wanna show you how a queen is supposed to be treated."

"I like the sound of that," I said as I rubbed my foot against his leg under the table. He started smiling.

"Why you playing, shorty?"

"I like to play."

"So do I."

"You wanna play with me, Mario?"

"I would love to but we can wait on that. It ain't no rush, is there?"

"No, I guess not," I said a little disappointed. I have never been shot down like that by no nigga. Maybe he wasn't attracted to me. Or maybe he was making me wait for a reason. We finished eating and left.. He dropped me off at home and told me to call him tomorrow after work. He was gonna pick me up and take me out to eat.

I got in the house and turned my phone back on. I had it off for at least three hours. That was a new record. As soon as it powered back on, Jay called. "What's up, baby?" I said sounding innocent.

"Where you been, boo? You had me worried about you."

"I was at Shannon's house, Jay."

"Hmmm. I see you still hanging around with that dyke bitch. She still eating your pussy like she did at the movies?"

"If she was, she would be doing it right now," I shot back at him.

"Yeah, get fucked up if you want."

"I see you're still the same. Look, what's up?"

"Sorry. I don't want you to think I'm still the same. You feel like coming out?"

"And do what? I have to work tomorrow."

"Nothing just come outside for a few minutes. I got something for you."

"Where are you?"

"Outside."

"I'm coming." I went outside and he was leaning against the car. It was so quiet outside it was creepy. You would think that it being a summer night, people would be outside but I guess not. "Hey, baby," I said kissing him and hugging him.

"What's up with you? You're looking good."

"Thank you," I replied twirling around. "So what you got for me?"

"Damn, chill out," he said laughing. He reached in the car and pulled out a long box. I opened it and inside was a single glass rose with a note attached to it. I flipped the note over and read it:

'I love you and I'm sorry for everything I have done. Be my boo again. Love Jermaine'

I looked up at him with teary eyes and said 'yes.' That was so sweet of him. He pulled me into his arms and kissed me passionately. We eventually pulled away and he told me to go in the house. I did as I was told and went back inside. I sat the rose on my dresser next to my senior picture. I texted 'thank you' to him with a kissy face emoji. He texted back the same emoji. I received a text from Mario telling me good night. I texted back likewise. I liked Mario but I loved Jay. At least, I think I did. That's what I keep saying in my head. Nevertheless, Mario and I are just friends. Jay is my man. I was a little happy but still confused about what I wanted. I liked having my friends and having my old thing back.

Nymphopervtress

Chapter Nine:
Double Time

⸱⸱⸱❦⸱⸱⸱

It has been a slow day at work. I have been here since ten and it was two o'clock now. I got off in three more hours. I could have stayed home for all this. Nobody was even here. Jessica was off so it was boring anyway. It was me, John, and David, the delivery driver. Of course David was gone most of the day because people wanted their food delivered to their workplace. That wasn't cool because that left me with minimal to do. I was mostly on my phone. John had called me into his office as soon as I had finished sending a text to both Jay and Mario.

"Hey, boss," I said as I walked into his office. I couldn't understand how he survived in here. It was so cramped and majority of the room was taken up by papers. I don't know why he just didn't have a file cabinet. It wasn't my business but I just wondered.

"I see you're experiencing the boring part of the job," he said laughing. I didn't find the humor in it at all.

"Yeah. I thought it was always busy in here."

"It is. Mainly on the weekends though. I forgot to mention that part."

"Yeah, you kind of left that piece out. But not to be rude, what did you call me in here for?"

"Well, I wanted to talk to you. How do you like working here so far?"

"It's cool. I've only been here for a few weeks. I can't really judge it just yet."

"Thanks for the honest answer, Desiree. I am looking to hire an assistant manager. I don't wanna hire an outsider but I wouldn't mind promoting somebody."

"Cool."

"I was thinking about promoting you."

"Me? Already? I mean, I'm flattered but I haven't even been here that long."

"I know but I have been paying attention to you. Very close attention," he said as he came from behind the desk and stood in front of me. "You get a five dollar raise and paid time off for vacation and sick leave."

"That sounds good."

"How bad do you want it?"

"Hell, I could use that money."

"What are you willing to do for that raise?" I looked at him oddly.

"I know I would have to work harder and keep up my good work habits."

"You're absolutely right. How about starting now," he said unzipping his pants.

"What are you doing, John?"

"I'm helping you get that promotion you want. You do want it, right?"

"Yes, I do."

"Show me."

I asked that he put a condom on first. He went into his desk and pulled out a rubber. He quickly put it on and stood back in front of me. I placed his little penis in my mouth and sucked it. I was playing a good role as if I were really enjoying it. No doubt in my mind that he wasn't.

"Oh yes, suck that dick, baby. I like how that pretty little mouth feels. Get it hard for me, Desiree. I wanna get a little bit of your sweet young pussy."

I rolled my eyes but continued to suck him off. Just then my phone went off. It was Jay calling. I told him to call me at three because that's when I was going on my break. I stood up and moved away from John. "Hey, Jay. What's up love?"

"At work, dealing with these idiots. How's work going?"

"Work is good. I got a promotion."

"Already? That's my girl."

John was coming towards me. He pulled me by the hand and took me over to his desk. He unbuttoned my pants and dropped them and my thong to the floor. He bent me over and stuck his puny little penis inside me. If I didn't know any better, I would have thought he was using a piece of Vienna sausage or something to penetrate me. "Jay, how's your day going?" I asked, so I wouldn't be quiet too long on the phone.

"It's going aight, I guess. I just wanna see you tonight. You need a ride after work?"

"Naw, I'm good on the ride, boo. But I can't wait to see you tonight either."

"Cool. Well I'm gonna let you get back to work. Just text me. Love you."

"You, too. Bye." I hung up. I was so into the phone conversation I didn't even know John was finished. That was a crock of bullshit.

"Well, how was it?" he asked me.

"If you have to ask then you must don't think it was good."

"I know I put it down."

"Right."

I reached over and grabbed some napkins off his desk to clean up. I didn't even come. That shit was so weak. In my head, I thought, ain't no way he has a wife or kids. He told us he did but I didn't know how. I couldn't even feel anything so I knew for damn sure his wife didn't either. I fixed my clothes and went back out to the front and sat down. At least I got a promotion out of this.

Mario texted me telling me that he couldn't wait to see me in a little bit. I texted back I couldn't wait either. It was almost five so it wouldn't be long now.

****

Mario took me out to Jasper's for dinner. I loved this place! I ordered my usual Cajun chicken and shrimp entrée. We ate and talked and just enjoyed each other's company. Not once did the subject of sex come up. That was weird. Whenever Jay and I talked, we always mentioned sex or a sexual activity. This was like a breath of fresh air. I didn't even want this to end. I wish I didn't have to meet up with Jay later on tonight. I would have stayed the rest of the night with Mario, talking.

Mario took me back home and we sat in the parking lot a few minutes. I received a text from Jay saying he would be here in an hour. At least, I wouldn't get caught up again.

"What you doing tomorrow, shorty?"

"Not sure. I'm off again tomorrow. Can I see you?"

"I would love that but I gotta run up to New York to pick up a package. But to make it up to you, imma give you this." He handed me an envelope full of fifties. Oh my god.

"You want me to hold this for you?"

He threw his head back laughing. "Naw, naw, naw, baby girl. I want you to take this money and go out and enjoy yourself. Go pick up a few dresses and shit you think I would like to see you in. when I get back, imma come scoop you and you can crash at my house. I want you to give me a private fashion show."

"Aww, boo," I said hugging him and giving him a kiss. Our first kiss. Was a little different from kissing Jay but it was cool. Mario was spoiling me and I was loving every minute of it. I was gonna enjoy this. Hopefully, Jay never finds out because I wanna reap the benefits of being around a hustler.

"That was a nice kiss. Maybe I should send you shopping more often," he said laughing. "But on the real if you gonna be kicking it with me and being my girl, you gotta be looking good at all time. You already do but you can never have too much. You know what I'm saying?"

"Yes."

"Good. Now go on inside and take a picture for your man to have as a screen saver."

"What if you be around Jay and he sees it?"

"I'm not worried about that nigga and neither should you."

"Okay." I really did have to worry about him. Especially if I'm supposed to be his girlfriend. I went in the house and took a quick shower. I changed into some sweats and a half shirt. I grabbed clothes for tomorrow and stuffed the envelope in my top drawer. No need in chancing Jay finding it in my bag. He called and said he was outside and I went out to meet him..

He had taken me to a hotel in Virginia. It was a nice little room at the Holiday Inn. As soon as we got in the room, we went at each other. We were rougher than usual. We knocked over the lamp on the nightstand and everything trying to make our way to the bed. We tore at each other's clothes until we both were completely nude. He picked me up and fucked me up against the wall. It felt like a steel pipe was going in and out of my pussy as his thick dick went all the way up in my guts. We were only able to do that position because he had come rather quickly. When we finished, we cuddled. "I'm so glad we decided to try this again, Desiree."

"Me too," I said in a low tone. "Hey, I wanna go shopping tomorrow, Jay."

"Oh really? Now? How much money you need, baby?"

"Doesn't matter, boo. Whatever you give me will do."

He reached in his wallet and pulled out two crisp one hundred dollar bills. "Here you go."

Was he serious? I thought to myself. His dick was long and so was his tongue. I guess his money wasn't. At least not long enough for me. "Thanks, baby." I went to put the money in my bag and laid back down. He turned on ESPN to watch the highlights. That was my cue to kiss him goodnight and go to sleep because I didn't wanna watch that shit. I did just that and drifted off to sleep thinking about Mario. I might have to choose him over Jay. Mario was a gentleman. He didn't wanna rush into having sex with me and he already spoiled me to the max. Is this what love was? Jay surely wasn't a gentleman. He always flipped out about something. He said he'd changed but he still came off as a little wolf in sheep's clothing. It just hadn't shown up again yet. But it was coming soon. I could feel it. Until then, I was going to enjoy playing both sides.

Chapter Ten:
End Of The Road

❧

I was getting showered with gifts and money left and right when it came to Mario. I told my sister, Shanice, I had a new boo. I just didn't disclose who it actually was. I told her his name was Ronnie and she believed me and left it at that. I loved everything about Mario and I still ain't give him any cookies yet. That was the good thing about it. I was getting tired of Jay, honestly. We had been in a few more fights within the past couple of weeks. Mario had seen the bruises when we were in the shower one morning.

"What the fuck happened to your neck, Desiree?"

"Don't even trip, boo. Some little bitch was hating on me and we got into a little scuffle. That's all. No biggie, Bae." In all actuality, Jay had choked me and left fingerprints on my neck. But I couldn't tell him that since I had been telling him Jay and I haven't seen each other.

"Yeah, okay. Don't make me have to fuck a bitch up. I can bust a cap in her, too."

"Calm down, Baby. Fuck that bitch. I handled it myself."

"Aight, Shorty." That was the end of that conversation.

I was sitting around thinking while Mario was out on the block for a little while. I really liked Mario and Jay was a big road block in this situation. I received a text from Mario while I was deep in thought:

Mario: Wyd baby girl?

Me: Thinking.

Mario: I hope you thinking about me as much as I'm thinking about you right now.

Me: I surely am. I was thinking about us going to the next level.

Mario: A relationship?

Me: Yes.

Mario: If you ready, then let's do it. I had been waiting for you to say that, baby.

Me: So you're officially my boyfriend now?

Mario: You damn right. And your man will be home in a couple hours and I'm hungry.

Me: Okay, baby. I will make dinner for you no problem.

Mario: Cool. Btw I wanted to confirm something. You can cook, right? Like, I will see tomorrow, right? Lol

Me: Oh, you got jokes? How about you starve?

Mario: naw, baby. I'm just kidding. I'll see you in a couple hours.

Me: okay.

That boy was so damn crazy. Talking about can I cook? Pssh he knew better than that. I decided to cook him steak smothered in onions and a baked potato. He would think he was at a restaurant fucking around with my culinary skills. Before I started, I texted Jay. He texted back soon after:

Me: hey, Jay

Jay: What's up baby? Wyd?

Me: Just chilling. I wanted to tell you something.

Jay: What's that?

Me: I think we should break up. I'm not happy.

Jay: You joking right? Nobody breaks up with Jermaine. I do the breaking up

Me: yeah, along with breaking arms and shit too. Trust me, I know.

Jay: you know what? Fuck you then! You ain't nothing but a little hoe any fucking way. I don't know why I even wanted to fuck back with your little dumbass anyway.

Me: Yeah, idk either. Maybe because I got good pussy.

Jay: you mean had. Your pussy has been like a damn city bus since I bust your lil ass open. Everybody's getting to ride that pussy. I was just the main passenger. Now you can let other niggas get a piece of it too.

I didn't even respond back. It was no need to. He was being ignorant as always because his little feelings were hurt. Fuck that nigga! Because at the end of the day he ain't give a fuck about me. He didn't do shit with me but fuck me and beat me. Damn sure wasn't gonna miss that. It was just the end of the road for Jay and I. Now I was gonna see where the road with Mario by my side would take me. I finished that shit with Jay now it was time to make dinner for my man.

I put the steak on low as I chopped up some onions and peppers. I put the baked potatoes in the oven and kept a close eye on them so they wouldn't overcook. Mario was going to love this. Especially since it was my first time cooking for him. I decided to make corn on the cob and biscuits to go with the meal. Nothing made a man happier than a sexy woman that was smart and could cook. I checked the time and it was close to nine. Mario would be home any minute. I had to hurry up and finish my presentation.

I heard the key in the door as soon as I finished lighting the candles. He came in and I yelled, "Surprise."

He walked over to me with his mouth agape. "What is all this, Boo?"

"I just wanted to cook you a nice meal, Baby. I wanted to show you how much I care about you and appreciate you."

"I know that's right. I love a woman who takes care of her man."

"Go wash your hands while I fix our plates. Hurry up so your food don't get cold."

He walked steadfastly to the bathroom down the hall. He washed his hands and came back with quickness. He sat at the head of the table like he always did and waited patiently. I came back carrying both of our plates and sat them on the table. "Who told you I liked steak?"

"Lucky guess. I hope you like it."

"I'm sure I will as long as it doesn't have me on the toilet all night," he said laughing.

"Shut up," I said playfully punching him in the arm. We sat and ate dinner while he told me all about his day. His day was always full of something. Mine is just full of rude customers and nasty ass pizza. I enjoyed hearing about his lifestyle. It was dangerous and sexy to me. We finished eating and I told him I wanted to go to bed early.

"That's cool. I'm gonna just chill and watch a little TV."

"Okay," I said. I knew he was gonna say that which was good. I went upstairs and took a nice hot shower. When I got out, he was still downstairs. I moisturized my skin with my baby oil gel and tiptoed over to the closet. I pulled out a black negligee and a black sheer cover up. I had been practicing wearing higher heels all week long and I was now confident enough to walk in them for my man. I held the heels in my hand and slowly and quietly went down the stairs. He was still watching TV and he couldn't see me behind him. I slipped on the heels and walked over to the wall that separated the living room and kitchen.

"I never said I wanted to go to bed alone, Mario," I said seductively.

He turned around and saw me and his mouth dropped open. I walked over there as sexy as ever and sat on his lap. "Wow, Baby. What's the special occasion?"

"No special occasion, Hun. I just thought I would put on something nice for you. And I was hoping this would get you to come up to bed with me. I hate sleeping alone," I said as I laid my head on his shoulder and rubbed my hand across his chest.

"Why we gotta go up to the bed? You here right now so we might as well sleep here."

"Yeah, we could," I said standing up. "Or you can carry me up to the bedroom."

"That sounds even better." He scooped me up in his arms and carried me up the stairs to his room. He laid me on the bed and took off his shoes and shirt. He exposed a chiseled body covered in tattoos. It reminded me so much of how 50 Cent's body had looked. My mouth watered a little bit.

He walked to the foot of the bed and knelt onto the bed. He slowly kissed up my calf muscle making his way up to my thighs. He didn't even bother to take my heels off. "I've been waiting for this moment, Baby. I wanna cherish it. I wanna make love to you like it's gonna be the last time," he said before pulling my thong to the side and gently licking my pussy. He started slow and it was giving me shivers. He sped up his tongue a little and I moaned. He stuck in one finger. Then two. Then three. "Aahhh," I yelled. He did a come here motion inside me and I lost it. I pulled him up towards me and kissed his lips. They were so soft and chocolaty. I bit on his bottom lip and sucked it into my mouth. "Take your pants off, baby."

He stood up and dropped his pants to the floor. His dick was already erect and trying to jump out his boxers. I sat up on the side of the bed in front of him. I pulled him towards me and took all of him in my mouth. I gagged a little but it was worth it. I had to please my man and make sure he was taken care of sexually. I stopped sucking and looked up at him. "I want you to fuck my face, daddy."

"You want me to do what now?"

"I said fuck my face." He put my head in between his hands and I put his dick back in my mouth. He moved my head back and forth on his dick as I sucked and slurped up my saliva. I gripped his shaft as I sucked and started moving faster and trying to put his entire dick down my throat. He was enjoying it. I could tell as he put his hand on top of my head and continued to fuck the shit outta my mouth. I pulled his dick out and spat on it and stroked it some more. He couldn't take it no more. He pushed me back on the bed but I interjected. "You lie down and let me go for a ride."

"You sure you can handle this ride, little lady?"

"I think I can," I replied as I hopped on his dick. I moaned as soon as it got all the way into my stomach. I rolled my hips back and forth. I moved my ass in a circle formation and he went wild. He grabbed me by the waist and rammed that dick up in me. I locked my fingers on the back of his neck and held on so I wouldn't fall off of this roller coaster ride. We continued in that position until he slowed his pace. I jumped off and went back to sucking him off. He pushed down on the back of my head to make it go in deeper. I kicked off my heels and got into the doggy style position. "I want you to fuck me like this Daddy," I said.

"I don't mind, Shorty," he said kneeling, getting behind me. He kissed

Nymphopervtress

my back and licked all the way down my spine until he reached the top of my ass crack. He grabbed my ass and bit down gently. I moaned out loudly. He stuck his tongue inside my asshole and penetrated it and licked it. He put his thumb in my hole as he inserted his penis inside my vagina. He fucked me so hard and deep I was scared to come. I thought if I did I was gonna pass out. I felt him pull his dick and thumb out at the same time. Then I felt a slight pain as he pushed the head of his penis inside my asshole. I jumped a little but he held me by the waist. "Be cool, Baby. I'm not gonna hurt you. I'm gonna take my time. If you don't wanna do it, we don't have to."

"I do but I'm not ready, Boo. Don't be mad."

"Mad about what? It's cool. We can do it whenever you ready."

"Thanks." He got back inside my pussy and fucked me until we both had come. We laid next to each other, panting, trying to catch our breath. "That was amazing," I said throwing my arm across his sweaty chest.

"Yeah, that was. And so are you."

"Thank you, Baby," I said leaning and giving him a quick peck on his lips.

"See that's how we ended up in the sheets the last time."

I laughed. "Oh, yeah? Who's to say I wasn't trying to start up another round?"

"Oh, we can. Don't think just because I'm a few years older I can't keep up."

"We'll see about that, Pops," I said laughing.

"Oh, I got your Pops," he said as he pulled the cover over top of us and got back on top of me. We ended up making love again until the wee hours of the morning.

Chapter Eleven:
Moving Out

It has been like a whirlwind romance between Mario and I. There have been non-stop shopping, dining out, hanging out around the house, date nights, and most of all, love-making. I haven't even thought about Jay's ass. He never even crossed my mind. I was loving these past couple of months. I have been doing nothing but going to work and coming back to Mario's house every night. I was actually home for a change today, but only for a little while. I wanted to see Jessica and Shannon and get some more clothes for work and stuff next week. We were lying around in my room just chilling.

"So what's been going on with you and Mario?" Jessica asked.

"Since you wanna be nosey, we have been kicking it. I enjoy being around him."

"Did you enjoy being around Jay?"

"Yes and no. I can honestly do without Jay and his bullshit."

"What if that's how Jay feels about you?" Shannon said speaking up. I almost forgot she was even there. She was so damn quiet.

"What the hell is that supposed to mean?" I shot back at her.

"What I mean is didn't you fuck around on him? He probably didn't wanna get hurt by you again. Did you ever think about that?"

"Yeah, I did and I apologized for what I did. He never apologized for what he did. So again, I'm glad I don't have to deal with Jay and his bullshit," I said, as I raised my voice of few octaves.

"Ladies calm down," Jessica interjected. "Shannon we should be happy for Desiree."

"I probably would be if she wasn't messing around with Jay's cousin."

"I don't think it really matters. They both are grown and they chose to be together and be happy."

"Thank you," I said to Jessica. I rolled my eyes at Shannon and she rolled hers back. I don't understand what her deal was about Mario and I being together but I didn't like it.

I got up and packed some clothes. I couldn't wait to go back to Mario's house. I loved being there except when I had to go to work or he had to go to work or go on business trips. I would feel lonely at times and be tempted to reach out to someone for comfort. I didn't wanna do that to Mario but temptation was a bitch. But so was karma.

I sat back down and grabbed my phone to call Mario. He answered on the second ring.

"What's up, baby girl?"

"Hey, baby. Where are you?"

"On my way to you."

"Great. I can't wait to see you."

"Same here. You need anything before I come get you? Did you eat already?"

"No. I was waiting for you. We could go grab some Chipotle or Panda Express if you want."

"Shit, we might get both. A nigga hungry as a damn hostage," he laughed.

"You just greedy that's all. That big breakfast I made you this morning and you talking about being hungry. All you wanna do is eat."

"Yeah, you right about that. But all I really wanna eat is you, Baby."

I blushed on the phone. "You're so nasty."

"And you love it."

"I don't know about all that," I said, laughing into the phone.

"I will be outside in a few minutes so be ready to come out. Tell your girls they gotta go. You got plans with your man," he said, laughing into the receiver.

"I'll be out in two," I said.

"Okay. See you soon," he hung up and I went to go kick my girls out.

We all walked outside together and just stood there talking a bit while I waited all of five seconds for my boo to pull up. They all said hello to one another and the girls left as I got in the car with Mario. I got in the car and kissed him. "You ready to go?"

"No, Mario. I wanted to ask you something before we drove off."

"What's on your mind, Boo?"

"Well, you know I have been coming over your house all the time and I'm barely here. I was just thinking-"

"Thinking you should just move in with me?" he said finishing my sentence.

"Yeah, something like that. Well, what do you think?"

"Shit! Hell yeah! You can move in. You make me breakfast every morning, you take care of my needs every night, and you suck my toes," he said laughing. "I would be honored to have you move in with me, Desiree."

"Aww thanks, Baby. I gotta tell my mom."

"You can tell her later. Right now we gotta get the rest of your things. Better yet, fuck that. I will buy you all new shit. You can keep that stuff here for when you visit."

"Okay, cool." He put the car in drive and we were on our way to his home. Excuse me, I meant our house. I liked the way that sounded.

****

We arrived at the house and he helped me take my duffel bag in the house while I grabbed our food and drinks. He dropped the bag right by the door and took the other bags out my hand.

"You're so helpful," I said looking at him and grinning.

"Well, you know how I do," he said rubbing on his goatee.

"You know what movie you wanna watch, Babe?" I asked as I slipped off my shoes and walked to the living room with the drinks.

"Yeah. For some reason I wanna watch Halloween."

"Are you serious?"

"Yeah, what's wrong with that?"

"Michael Myers is my favorite!" I said ecstatically.

"Get the fuck outta here. That's my shit!" he exclaimed.

"So are we gonna start from the very first one?"

"It wouldn't be right if we didn't."

"True statement." We sat back and ate our food and enjoyed each other's company. We were almost done eating and halfway through the movie when somebody knocked at the door.

"Were you expecting company, Babe?" I asked Mario.

"Naw, Boo. You sure it ain't your girls? If it is, we can have some fun," he said rubbing his hands together and smiling like a damn Chester cat.

"Negro please. They don't want you. They wouldn't come unannounced nor do they even know where you live."

"Go see who it is, Baby," he said reaching for his burner under the sofa.

I walked over to the door and looked through the peephole. Oh shit! It was Jay. He started knocking harder and I jumped. I tiptoed back over to where Mario was. "It's Jay," I whispered.

"Oh, damn. Look, go upstairs and chill in the bedroom. I will get rid of him as fast as possible.

"Okay, Babe," I said. I gave him a quick kiss and went up the steps in a hurry to the bedroom. I heard him open up the door for Jay. I cracked the bedroom door open so I can eavesdrop on their conversation.

"What's up, Dawg," I heard Jay say as he dapped up Mario.

"Ain't nothing much. Just cooling."

"I see," I could tell he was in the living room from the direction his voice was coming. "I see you not cooling it alone. Who you got up in here, lil cuz?"

"Well, you know how I roll."

"Yeah, I do. So my question should've been how many you got up in here."

"You real funny," Mario said laughing. From what I was hearing, I didn't hear shit that was funny at all. "I just got one girl here, bruh."

"That's cool. Who is it?"

"Damn you nosey, cuz."

"It's that girl, Shanice ain't it?"

"Naw, man. It's somebody else."

"You still talking to Lexi? She told me she hit you up the other day to chill and you told her you was busy."

Lexi? Who the fuck is Lexi? I was gonna get in his ass when I went downstairs for sure.

"Naw man. It ain't Lexi. I don't mean to rush you, my nigga, but what the hell did you want?"

"Oh yeah, shit, my bad. We gotta take a trip in a few days up to Pennsylvania to meet up with the connect. They got a shipment coming in and we gotta go re-up."

"Aight, cool. I just gotta let my girl know."

"Your girl? Lil cuz finally settling down?"

"Settling? Naw, dawg, not me," he said laughing.

"Well when do I get to meet the little lady? Can I meet her today?"

"Naw, man. She's upstairs getting ready for, Daddy. She said she had a surprise for ya boy."

"Oh shit true. My bad. Imma let you get back to your shorty, son. Imma hit you up in a couple of days so we can get shit arranged for the following day."

"Cool. Peace." I heard the door close and I went downstairs. "That was close," Mario said when I got to the bottom of the steps. I had my arms folded across my chest. "What's wrong, Boo?"

"Ain't no damn 'what's wrong, boo', Mario. Who the fuck is, Lexi?"

"She just some little bitch I used to run through. She a nobody."

"It sure didn't seem like she was a nobody. You was in here laughing it up about her. And she hit you up the other day? How come I didn't know about that?"

"Because it's none of your fucking business."

"I will keep that in mind."

"Keep what in mind?"

"That we keeping secrets from each other now."

"Oh yeah? Well fuck it! You ain't gotta believe me. I told you that bitch is a nobody. If you wanna trip about it then that's your business."

"Fine. I will." I grabbed my duffel bag and my food.

"Where are you going, Desi?"

"If you must know I'm going upstairs. I'm gonna sleep in one of the other rooms. I don't wanna be near your lying ass."

"Suit yourself," he said and stormed off. He went back to the sofa and finished the movie and eating. I stomped up the stairs and locked myself inside the room. I didn't wanna be near his ass but then I did. No fuck that. I thought to myself. His ass wasn't getting no booty tonight. Imma give his ass time to think about what the fuck he had done. I hoped deep down inside me that this was just a bump and not gonna be a mountain in this relationship. I'm hoping I didn't make a big mistake moving in with him.

Chapter Twelve:
Three Times In A Row

❧❧

The day had finally come when it was time for Mario to leave for a few days. I was glad so I could be alone. I was thinking about getting a little payback. He wanna go messing around with other bitches then I'm gonna go around and have some fun too. Deep down, I dreaded him leaving. It was only for a few days but I didn't know what I was gonna do.

"Hey, Boo, you up?" Mario said from the other side of the bedroom door. Ever since the other day, I haven't come out of the room except when he was out working the streets. I haven't seen him, spoke to him, or sexed him. And I was damn sure missing him and his body. But I was standing my ground. "I see you still ignoring me, huh? Well, I'm about to leave for Pennsylvania. Desiree? Do you hear me, Baby? Anyway, I left you some money on the table with your copy of the house keys. I will be back in three days. Just call me if you need anything. I will have Rocko bring you whatever you need if you don't feel like going anywhere. I love you, Boo." That was the last thing I heard before I heard his footsteps going down the steps. I got up and looked out the window. He was getting in the car with Jay. He looked up at the window to the room I was in. I guess he wanted me to wave him off but that wasn't gonna happen.

I had texted Jessica and Shannon to see if they wanted to come over. They both said yeah and they would be over in a little bit. Until then, I needed to find something to do. I got on the internet and googled online dating networks. So many came up and I chose this site called Tagged. I created my account and within seconds, I was able to chat with people everywhere. I looked through the pictures and were turned on to some and turned off to others. They had straight, gay, bisexual, trannys, everything! I had inboxed this real cute guy that had dreads. His name was Lamar. Not sure if that was his real name or his screen name nor did I care. He was a little husky type of guy but he was handsome and rugged. He didn't live that far from here either. Maybe we could link up later.

I was having fun on Tagged. I was sending and receiving messages from guys and girls. A couple of bisexuals were in my inbox too. I didn't swerve them. I welcomed them too. I was just a girl looking to have some fun. I was determined to teach Mario a lesson about trying to fuck with me. He had me fucked all the way up!

I heard a car pull up outside. It was Jessica, Shannon, and Scott. What the hell was he doing here? This was not going to be pretty. I ran down the steps to open the door before they reached the porch.

"Girl, you running like you being chased by the feds," Jessica said laughing. They walked past me into the foyer then to the living room.

"Not funny. What the hell are you doing here, Scott?" I asked him.

"I wasn't invited to the party?"

"There isn't any party."

"Hell three pretty girls and me by myself. That sounds like a party to me."

"Don't call me pretty and don't include me in that scenario. I don't like niggas," Shannon snapped.

"My bad. You right, Shannon. We could get Jessica and Desiree to give us some booty."

"That's more like it," Shannon said smiling. Her and Scott dapped each other up. I stood there shaking my head, laughing.

"Well what y'all wanna do?" I asked everybody.

"How bout we throw a party?" Jessica said excitedly.

"That sounds fun. Who we gonna invite?"

"Leave that to me," Jessica replied as she pulled out her phone and started typing a thousand words a minute.

"We gonna have to go get some food," Shannon replied.

"All you think about is food, Shannon."

"And pussy," she said cheesing.

"Anyway, take this money and get some snacks and drinks for tonight," I said, handing Jessica two hundred dollar bills. She took it and her and Shannon left.. Why didn't they take Scott's ass with them? Oh well, I guess it wasn't no harm in him staying.

"So I see now why you haven't been hitting me up, Desi," Scott said walking towards me.

"What are you talking about?"

"You missing me."

"Yeah, I guess I miss hanging out with you."

"Oh yeah? Well let's see," he said pulling me into a tight embrace and kissing me. I was kissing back so I was just as guilty. I could feel my pussy awaken as well as my breasts. They looked like they were trying to bust out my shirt. He took my shirt off and pulled my bra straps down. He buried his face in between my breasts like he wanted to be smothered. I moaned as he sucked my nipples like a newborn baby. He was sucking so hard I thought I was breastfeeding him! I pushed him away and unbuckled his jeans. They dropped to the floor and I dropped to my knees. I was sucking the shit out of his dick. I missed having a dick in my mouth. Since I have been mad at Mario the past few days, I haven't been pleased or pleased him. So I was gonna take advantage of this now.

I stopped sucking and stood up. I took my sweat pants off and grabbed Scott's hand and led him to the kitchen. I hopped up on the counter and he put his dick inside of me after we adjusted the position a little. He was holding me by the waist and thrusting his dick up in my pussy as I held onto the counter for dear life. He started going faster and kept it up until we both came. That was so good. Made me wonder why I stopped fucking him. Other than the fact about me being with Mario, I didn't know why. I told him to stay downstairs while I went to go take a shower and get ready for tonight. Shannon and Jessica would be back in any given minute.

****

The party was jumping. I knew Jessica knew a lot of people but goddamn! The living room was packed from wall to wall. I'm glad Mario doesn't have any valuables in here. I thought to myself. Everybody was having fun. I was even having fun. I had been dancing with this guy named JoJo for about an hour. He was grinding on me and he was making my pussy hotter than it should have been. Once I made sure everybody was good, he and I snuck off to the walk-in closet in the upstairs hallway.

"Where are we going?" JoJo asked.

"Just follow me," I said.

We got to the top of the stairs and it seemed like we were in an entirely different place. Nobody was allowed upstairs so it seemed deserted. This was good. I pulled him into the closet and started tearing at his clothes. I started kissing him all over and grabbing every part of his body. "Do you have a condom?" I asked him.

"Yeah, I do."

"Good. Give it to me." He handed me the condom and I opened the wrapper. "Lay down on the floor," I said.

"The floor?"

"Yes, the floor," he just stood there. I was about to get mad. I turned on the light and waited for my eyes to adjust to the lighting. I saw a blanket on the top shelf and pulled it down. I laid it on the floor then he laid down.

"Pull your pants off," I instructed. He pulled them down to under his butt and I pulled them all the way down to his ankles. I pulled his dick through the slit in his boxers. I massaged it to make it a little harder before I put the condom on. It was easy to get it in quick since I was wearing a skirt tonight. I purposely did that for this specific reason. I didn't even have on any panties. I hopped on top of him and rode his dick. It was deep enough for me to feel it but not how I felt Mario's. I rubbed on his chest and he held onto my waist. We fucked for about twenty minutes before we both had come in unison.

"That was good," JoJo said as he was straightening up his clothes.

"Thanks. So were you," I said. I fixed my skirt and looked out into the hallway. The coast was clear so we left. He went back to the party and I went to the bathroom. "I will meet you back downstairs."

"Okay." I went to go pee and to flush the evidence. I washed my sweet area and it felt good. It had a tingly feeling that I always endure after a good helping of penis. I loved that feeling. I looked at myself in the mirror and smirked. "Mario don't know what the fuck he missing out on. Imma let him keep playing games and so am I," I said aloud to myself in the mirror. I left the bathroom and went back downstairs. The party was still live and I was looking for my next victim.

****

The party was finally over and the house was back to clean. Thanks to Jessica, Shannon, and Scott, it didn't take long to put the house back in order. I was now back to being alone and horny again. I had some Patron and hit a few blunts and now I needed some dick to complete my night. I logged back into my Tagged account and Lamar had messaged me his number. Bingo. I got action. I instantly called him.

"Hey, Lamar."

"What's up? Who this?" he even sounded sexy.

"This is Miss D from Tagged. You had inboxed me your number."

"Oh yeah. I remember writing you. I was hoping you were gonna hit me up. What's up with you though?"

"Nothing really. I'm just lonely."

"What's a pretty girl like you doing lonely? I know you got niggas lined up around the block waiting for a chance to spend some time with you."

"Naw, I don't think so, Boo," I said, laughing into the phone. "I wanted to see you if you were available."

"Shit! For you? Yeah. But where your man at?"

"He's outta town. I'm glad he is too. I found out he was talking to other females."

"That's fucked up."

"Yeah, I know. But enough about him, where can we meet?"

"Well, I live on Southern Avenue. Where you live?"

"By Iverson Mall."

"You want me to come scoop you for a little bit?"

"Yeah. Meet me at Iverson Mall in ten minutes. I'll be the girl wearing the short blue jean skirt."

"Oh word? I definitely won't miss that."

"See you in a few minutes." I hung up the phone and ran to the bathroom. I had to make sure my makeup was beat and my hair was flawless. I looked great. I grabbed my little purse and put some condoms in it. I didn't know if he had any or not but I wanted to be prepared.

I was walking to the mall and all the guys were whistling at me. You would think that they had never seen a pretty young woman before. Or maybe it was the skirt that I had on. It was short and it made my thighs look more scrumptious. Yeah, that's what it was. Lamar called me and said he was there. He said he was in a black Chevy Malibu. I saw it across the street by the Bojangles and I told him I was coming. I jogged over to the opposite side of the street. I had stopped and bent over to fix the tongue on my Chucks and a guy behind me brushed up against me. I stood up and looked at the dude. He was looking too good to fuck up or cuss out so I just kept it moving.

I walked up to the black Malibu and smiled when the driver side window came down. I'm glad Lamar looked just like his picture. He got out the car and gave me a hug.

"What's up, Desiree?"

"Nothing much. Nice to meet you, Lamar."

"Likewise. You ready to go?"

"Yes."

"Where you wanna go?"

"Your place," I said whispering in his ear. I twirled around and strutted around to the passenger side. I got in and caught a glimpse of his smile. We drove to his house which really wasn't that far from the mall either. I was rubbing my hand all over his crotch as he drove. I could tell he was enjoying it too.

We pulled up to his house and drove up the driveway. The garage door opened with the push of a button and we drove inside. Before he even cut the car off, I climbed over the arm rest and sat on his lap. My back was towards him just how I wanted it to be. I grinded my hips on his lap and grabbed his hands to place on my breasts. He bit down into my flesh and I screamed out with pure pleasure dripping from my lips. He massaged my breasts and kissed on the back of my neck as I gyrated on him.

He moved the seat back some and told me to lean up. He took his dick out his pants and put on a condom that he had taken from out the glove box. He put it on and sat me back down on it. I bounced up and down as I held onto the steering wheel. Within minutes, he grabbed my waist and held me down as he came. It feels good to have guilty pleasures. I thought to myself.

"Wanna go again?" he asked.

"Naw, I'm good. We can hook up later in the week. I gotta get home and get some rest."

"That's cool."

I got off his lap and he handed me some napkins to clean myself up. He put his seat belt on, pushed the garage door button, and backed down the driveway. I gave him a little bit of head on the way to my house to show my appreciation for him giving me some good sex. He pulled up to the street where Mario and I lived on and I told him to drop me off on the corner.

"You sure you're good, Desiree?"

"Yeah I'm good."

"Cool. I really enjoyed meeting you."

"Likewise," I said. I leaned over and kissed him on the cheek before exiting the car. I stood there until he pulled off. Didn't need Lamar finding out where I lived. I walked to the house smiling knowing I had succeeded in my payback against Mario. That smile quickly vanished as soon as I opened the door.

"What's up, boo?"

Chapter Thirteen:

"You look like you just seen a ghost, Desiree," Mario said walking towards me.

"Hey, baby," I said walking towards him to give him a hug. "Why didn't you tell me you were on the way back?"

"I thought I would surprise you. Or a better question is, where are you coming from this time of night?"

"Oh, I was hanging out with Shannon and Jessica tonight. I hope you don't mind that they were here."

"Naw it's cool. But you were out dressed like that?"

"Yeah, what's wrong with it?"

"Nothing I guess."

"Ok, well give me a kiss." He kissed me on the lips. "I missed you."

"I missed you too, boo."

"That's good. Let me go hop in the shower and wash this all day stench off me. I know you need some pussy because I definitely need you."

"I'll be in the room waiting for you, Baby. Don't be too long please."

"I won't." I walked up the stairs and took a deep breath. I couldn't believe I almost got caught. I wasn't gonna be like Mario and get caught. I was starting to fall in love with Mario but that changed my whole perspective on everything. I stripped out my clothes and jumped in the shower. I scrubbed every inch of my body to the point where I thought I would rub my skin off. When I got out, I moisturized my body then went into the room with Mario. He was stretched out on the bed in the dark.

"You want the TV or something on, Hun?"

"No thanks. I just wanna make love to you and hold you all night. I missed that while I was gone. I missed you. I'm sorry, boo."

That's all I wanted to hear from him. An apology. Now I can get back to business with my boo. I walked over to him and laid beside him. He turned over and kissed me. He moved on top of me and started to make love to my body. We had been intertwined well into the wee hours of the morning. Once we had finally climaxed, I fell next to him on the bed.

"I'm sorry, Boo," I said to him.

"I'm sorry, too."

Nymphopervtress

I fell asleep in his arms just like it should always be.

****

I woke up to the smell of breakfast cooking. I went to the bathroom to use it and brush my teeth. I washed and dried my hands before heading downstairs. I got to the bottom of the steps and saw Mario in the kitchen, cooking in his boxers. I walked up behind him and grabbed him around the waist from behind.

"Morning, Boo," I said kissing his back.

He turned around and kissed my forehead. "Morning, sleepy head. How did you sleep?"

"I slept good. How about you?"

"Great. I had my girl by my side."

"Aww, that's so sweet. What you down here burning?" I asked, laughing.

"Burning? Girl, please. You know I can burn."

"Yeah, burn down somebody's damn house."

"Then you don't have to eat my burnt food, missy. You can eat frosted flakes and I'm gonna eat Belgian waffles," he said sticking his tongue out.

"I'm just joking, Babe. You know I love your cooking."

"You better," he said as he sat a plate down in front of me. Waffles, bacon and eggs decorated my plate. I didn't even know I was hungry until my stomach growled. I tore into the food after we both said grace.

"Damn, Baby. Slow down. You act like you haven't eaten in days."

"Sorry, Boo. I'm just really hungry that's all," I said, laughing and covering my mouth.

"You're good. I love a woman that loves to eat," he said rubbing on my thigh under the table.

We finished eating and went upstairs to relax. He rubbed my feet as we watched Criminal Minds—one of our favorite TV shows.

"You have to work today?"

"Yeah, I do, unfortunately."

"It's all good, Boo. You know you don't have to work there. Let me take care of you."

"You already do. And I appreciate it."

"No problem, sweetie."

I got up and walked to the bathroom. I think that breakfast was backing up on me. I was in there and my phone went off. Mario had brought it to me and I answered it in a whisper.

"Hello?"

"Hey, mama."

"Who is this?"

"Damn you talk to that many niggas, Boo? It's Lamar."

"Oh damn. Hey Lamar, what's up?"

"Nothing much. Just checking on you."

"I'm good. About to get ready for work."

"True. What time do you get off?"

"Ten."

"Need a ride?"

"Like last night?" I asked, smiling.

"I wouldn't mind it."

"Okay. I will text you the address at nine."

"Cool. Talk to you later."

I finished using the bathroom and walked back into the bedroom. As soon as I sat down on the bed, the questions came. "Who was that?"

"That was just Shannon giving me her new number."

"Oh okay."

Not sure if that was the answer he was looking for but it worked for me. I laid down and took a nap. I didn't plan on waking up until 2 o' clock.

****

I got to work and I walked right into the madness. It was packed inside the little front area and the phones were ringing off the hook. I saw Jessica and she was making three pizzas at a time. You go girl. I thought to myself. I looked for John and he was in the back. And he was actually doing work for a change.

"Hey John, I'm here," I said, when I caught his attention.

"I'm glad you're here, Desiree. Can you please help us out? The only person I'm glad that's here other than you is Jessica. If it weren't for her, we would be getting pummeled."

"I'm gonna go work the front."

"Okay."

I went to the front and made everyone get in one of the three open lines. If they were out of line, they would not be waited on. I guess they took heed to my warning because everybody did as I instructed and the loud ruckus turned to light murmurs. We were able to get all the phone orders and inside orders taken in an hour. After the rush was over, we were able to catch our breath for a second.

"So what happened to you last night?" Jessica asked me.

"What you mean?"

"Don't think I didn't notice you leave for about half an hour with JoJo. Where did y'all go?"

"We just went to talk," I lied.

"Sure you did. I know you and I know how JoJo can be. Watch yourself, baby girl."

What did she mean by that? I didn't have time to ask her because I was called into the office.

"What's up, John?"

"Great work today, Logan. I'm proud to have an employee like you."

"Uh thanks, John."

"Here you go." He handed me two envelopes. I opened the first one which was my paycheck for the last two weeks. Five hundred and twenty dollars. Not bad. I opened the other envelope and it was filled with cash. I counted it out. $800.

"What's the extra money for?"

"Well you did do extra work," he responded putting emphasis on the word extra.

"Um thanks." I didn't ask any questions. I just stuck an envelope in each one of my pockets and left his office. The day had seemed to go by fast and before I knew it, it was nine. I texted Lamar and told him I had forgotten my girlfriend was gonna pick me up. He understood and I told him I was gonna hit him up tomorrow. I texted Mario and told him to pick me up at ten. Knowing him, he was probably gonna be outside at 9:30.

We had cleaned up everything and I counted down the three registers and it was time to go. I was beat. I just wanted to go home, take a hot shower, and go to bed. I received a text from Mario saying he was outside. I didn't see him pull up nor did I see him parked outside. He probably parked around the corner. We locked up and I gave Jessica a hug before she got in her car. "Call me tomorrow, Desi. I'm off and I know you are too," she yelled out the driver side window.

"Okay, girlie," I said waving. I didn't even notice John behind me. I bumped right into him.

"My bad, John."

"It's cool. I like when you're close to me."

"Right," I said, walking to wherever Mario was.

"So when can you do some overtime?"

"What you mean?"

"When can I take you home and you do some extra work?"

"I'm not. I have a man."

"That's fine. But that's not answering the question at hand."

I rolled my eyes and walked away. I saw Mario's car parked two cars away from where I was. John pulled on my arm.

"What's it gonna take for you to give me some pussy? Everybody has a price."

"What the fuck? I'm not a fucking prostitute, John."

"Hell you should be. You would damn sure make more money than you do here."

"Leave me alone, John." I struggled to get my arm away from him but I failed.

"Is there a problem here?" We both looked and it was Mario. I hadn't even noticed him get out the car.

"Naw, it ain't. So mind your fucking business," John shot back at Mario.

"Well seeing as how this is my woman, she is my business. But I wanna know why you got your hands all over her."

"Oh I didn't know she had a man," he said releasing me and backing away.

"You're a fucking liar, John. I just told you that a few minutes ago when you were trying to get me to have sex with you for money."

"He did what?" Mario looked back and forth between John and me. Like a flash of lightning, Mario pulled out his nine and pointed it at John. He looked like he was about to shit on himself. "I'm gonna say this once and once only, you little bitch nigga. Stay away from my girl. If I catch you around her again, you and my friend gonna have a little convo. Got me?"

"I got you," John replied in a stutter. Mario grabbed my hand and we got in the car. I have never seen him angry. I wonder what he would do if he found out about all the mischief I was in for the past week.

"You're quitting that job, Desiree. You understand me?"

"Yes."

"Yes who?"

"Yes, Daddy."

Chapter Fourteen:

Doctor Visit

Today was the day I had a doctor visit. I hadn't told Mario I was going because I didn't want him to know. I had been burning for about a week now and I didn't know what the hell was going on. There was barely anybody here today, which was a good thing. I didn't like a lot of people around. I couldn't deal with them at a time like this.

"Desiree Logan," an older lady called aloud. I looked and it was the doctor's assistant, Marie. I had been coming here so long that I knew everyone here.

"Hey, Ms. Marie," I said as I stepped up on the scale to get weighed.

"How're you doing, Desiree?"

"Not good. I had to come get checked out. It burns a little when I pee."

"Oh wow. Okay. We will have to get a urinalysis and some blood work from you."

"That's fine."

She weighed me and then took me to a room. There, I waited for what seemed to have been forever but in actuality it was only twenty minutes.

"What brings you in today, Desiree?" Doctor Muhammad asked.

"Well I have been burning when I pee for about a week now. I'm not sure what it could be."

"Well that's what I'm here for. So I take it that you are having sex now?"

"Yeah I am," I said in a low tone.

"Don't be shy about it. We all do it."

I looked at him and wondered how big his dick was. I always had an attraction to him for some reason. "Yes I have been."

"How many partners?"

Hell I didn't know. I had to think about it. There was Scott, Mario, Jay, Lamar, JoJo, Jessica's father, and Shannon. I think that was everybody. Oh yeah and John. "I have had eight partners."

"Mmhmm," he said typing what I said. "How many of them have you had unprotected sex with?"

"Five."

He looked at me with a blank look. "Mmhmm, okay. I see. Well, I want you to go to the lab and put some urine in a cup and get some blood work done."

"Okay, but when will I get my results back?"

"In a few days."

"That's a long time to wait."

"I can rush the results and you can get them back in 24 hours."

"I would rather have that."

"Okay. I will give you a call sometime tomorrow."

"Okay." I walked to the lab and got my blood drawn. I then went to the bathroom and peed in a cup. I walked out of the doctor's office with my head held high but my mind was heavy. I couldn't understand why I had been so reckless and dangerous with my body. I should have been using protection every time. It might not be that bad. It may just be a yeast infection. Who am I kidding? It's AIDS. Oh dear god I have AIDS. This was not gonna be a good day after all.

I got home and Mario wasn't there. Good. I didn't feel like being bothered. I took all of my clothes off and got up in the bed. I had curled up into a fetal position and went to sleep.

I had been awaken by a thud. I jumped up out of my sleep and reached under the mattress for the small gun Mario had given me for protection when he wasn't there. I got out of the bed and gently walked out into the hall. It was dark downstairs except for one little dim light coming from the kitchen stove. I went down the stairs slowly with my gun leading the way. I peeped in the kitchen and saw a dark figure. I flipped on the switch and I shot at the ceiling. Mario turned around and looked at me. "What the hell are you doing, Desi?"

"My bad, Boo. I didn't know that was you. What the hell are you doing down here? You scared me."

"I was bringing something in the house for you," he said pointing to the living room. I walked over to the sofa and it was five shopping bags. I pulled the stuff out of the bags and there were heels, sneakers, dresses, jeans, and shirts. "What's all of this?"

"My sorry gifts to you. I blocked that girl, Babe. You don't have to worry about her anymore, okay?"

"Okay," I said. I walked back to where he was and hugged him tight. "I love you," I said.

"What did you just say?"

I couldn't believe what I had just said but it felt good to say. "I love you."

"I love you too, Desiree."

I grabbed the bags and he came over to assist me. We put the bags into the closet when we got in our room and I laid back down.

"What? No fashion show, love?" he said, laughing.

"Not tonight, Hun. I'm not feeling good."

"That's cool. I will just hold you. Would you like that?"

"I would love that." He took his clothes off and spooned with me under the covers. He fell asleep not long after midnight hit. I, on the other hand, was up thinking. What the hell have I done?

****

It was a bright early Wednesday morning. Another morning I wake up and Mario is gone. Of course he left a note as usual:
'went to make a trip up to New York. Be back tonight. Money is on the table. Left you the car keys. Ttyl love you. Mario'

I was used to this by now, really. If he wasn't going to Pennsylvania, he was going to either New York or Delaware. I hated the fact that he was a drug dealer sometimes. But on the upside, I didn't have to worry about trying to figure out what to tell him when I had to leave out in a few. I got up and showered. I just threw on some sweats for the day. I didn't really feel like looking glamorous today. I wasn't even gonna wear makeup today. Today was not gonna be a good day. I could feel it in my stomach. I wish I could lie in bed for the rest of the day but I couldn't. I had to put on my big girl drawers and go find out what was going on with my body.

I decided to eat a bowl of cereal. I didn't have much of an appetite either. I mean, who would? I received a call from the doctor's office after I finished cleaning the little bit of dishes out of the sink. They told me I could come in at any time before three. I grabbed the car keys and headed there.

"Well, Ms. Logan your results came back. And I regret to inform you that you have contracted chlamydia. It's a-" my mind went blank. I didn't hear anything after he said I had chlamydia. What the fuck? How stupid could you be, Desiree? I yelled at myself inside my head. I didn't even come back to reality until Doctor Muhammad shook me. "Are you okay?"

"No," I said dropping my head and crying. "What am I gonna do?"

"You're gonna face this. Its 100% curable, Desiree. You get a shot of antibiotics and cannot have sex for a full seven days. If you do, there is a chance that you can contract it again. All I can say is let your partners know so they can go get checked and as for you," he said placing a fatherly hand on my shoulder, "I want you to start being more careful."

"Yes, sir."

"Good. I will be seeing you, Desiree. Take care."

He left the room and the nurse came in. She gave me the shot of antibiotics and sent me on my way. No way in hell was I gonna tell all those people that I had gotten chlamydia. What would they say? What would Mario say? He was my main concern. He would find out that I had cheated and he would probably leave me. I really didn't have a choice. I had to tell him. I had to tell them all.

I decided to be a bitch and send everyone an individual text telling them to go get tested ASAP. Shannon didn't spaz on me but of course Jay and Scott did. I didn't bother telling the others since we didn't have unprotected sex. Jay and Scott called me all types of whores and bitches and sluts. It hurt me to the core that either of them would talk to me like that. They made it seem like I gave it to them. I should've been the one to get mad. I had caught it from one of them dirty motherfuckers, probably. I just turned all their messages on the 'do not disturb option.' I didn't have time for their shit. I had bigger fish to fry. I had to tell Mario. But how was I gonna break it to him?

Nymphopervtress

Chapter Fifteen:
We'll Get Through It

I had been walking around moping all day. I haven't eaten or drank anything. I have been down in the dumps since I got my results back. I still haven't even told Mario yet. He thinks I'm mad at him about something and he didn't even do anything. I didn't want him to feel like that because of my fuck ups. I went into his little 'man cave' as he called it.

"Mario."

"Hey, Boo. What's up?" he said, coming towards me.

"I'm sorry, Mario."

"Sorry for what?"

"I'm sick."

"Why are you sorry about that? I will take care of you."

"I have chlamydia," I said in a low tone.

"You have what?"

"I have chlamydia, Mario," I yelled at him and broke down crying.

"What the fuck? You were burning and you didn't even tell me? I thought we were better than that, Desiree," he said fuming.

"I'm sorry, boo. I didn't know. I just found out yesterday. I must have gotten it from when Jay and I were together. I don't know. I'm so sorry."

"It's okay," he said holding me tight in his arms. "It's just a misunderstanding. We'll get through this, baby. Okay?" I shook my head yes. "Have you had sex with anybody else, even when we started talking?"

I looked into his eyes. Now was the time to come clean. But I didn't. "No."

"Are you sure?"

"Well, Shannon and I had a little thing."

"What type of little thing?" he asked with a raised eyebrow.

"She ate me out."

"Seriously? And I missed it?" he said. He smiled and it made me smile. "We need to call her over right now so I can see this."

"I don't think so. We need to be calling you a doctor."

"That, too. I love you, baby," he said holding me again and kissing my forehead.

"I love you, too."

We left his private room and went to the bedroom. We couldn't have sex and he understood. So we just hung around the house all day long and ordered takeout. I was enjoying the time we were spending with each other. I don't know what I would do without him.

He had gone to take a shower. I was just relaxing, watching TV and his phone rang. I looked at the screen. It was a blocked number. I snatched up the phone and ran out the room with it.

"Hey, Baby. What you doing?" a female said on the other end of the phone.

"Baby? Bitch who you calling 'baby'?"

"Who the fuck is this?"

"This is Mario's girlfriend. Who the fuck is this?"

"Oh true. So you're the reason I have to block my number when I call?"

"Bitch, what?" This must be that hoe, Lexi. "What the fuck are you still doing calling my man, Bitch?"

"Better question is why does your man keep answering my calls? Tell him I will call him back or he can call me. You know, when you not around."

"Bitch I'm gonna always be around. You got me fucked up."

"Little girl, please."

"Little girl? Bitch I got your little girl," I said raising my voice.

"You don't wanna get fucked up, sweetheart."

"You ain't got the balls. Bitch, imma fuck you up when I see your ass in the streets."

"I know I ain't got the balls. I got the pussy and your man loves to be in it. Bitch." She hung up.

As soon as Mario came out the bathroom, I charged at his ass and knocked him down on the bed. I was pummeling him in the head throwing blow after blow. I was crying and yelling. I was infuriated.

"How the fuck could you do this to me?" I yelled.

"Desiree, calm down," he said trying to restrain me. "What is wrong now?"

"Your little bitch just called. Talking about you told her to block her number when she called."

"Babe, that bitch is lying. She's just mad because I cut her ass off."

"I can't tell. You know what? Prove it," I said handing the phone to him. "Call that bitch right now and tell her it's over and she better not call no more."

He blankly stared at me. What the fuck was I speaking?" A foreign language or something?

"Call her ass now, Mario."

"What is that gonna solve?"

"Call that bitch now or I'm walking."

"Okay, I'm gonna call her. Shit. Don't leave me, Baby." He dialed the number and she answered it.

"Put it on speaker."

"What your crazy bitch ass girlfriend doing answering your phone, Mario?" she yelled through the phone.

"Bitch, don't fucking play with me. I can hear your ass, Shawty. I already told you when I see you in the streets that ass is mine," I said.

"Well, it's only fair. I can share my ass with you too just like I do with your man, Bitch."

"Hold the fuck up now, Lexi. You know as well as I do, that I haven't been kicking it with you. If you don't stop hitting my phone and shit I'm gonna make your ass disappear for good. And you know I have the power to do so." It got silent on the other end. I could hear sniffling.

"I'm sorry Mario. I just really love you. I want you back."

"Bitch please. You don't love no fucking body. You didn't love me when you got that abortion did you? You didn't love me when you slept with my right hand did you? Fuck no! Your ass just loved what I could do for your lazy triflin' ass. Don't call my phone no more, Lexi. I'm serious and this is my last warning. Fall back. I'm happy now. Something you could have never made me." He hung up the phone.

I held him around his neck. "I love you, baby."

"I love you too, Desi. And I'm sorry. For everything."

"Me too. But we're a team, right?"

"Right."

"Exactly. So we're gonna get through these two little hiccups. We both did wrong and we admitted and fixed our wrongs. Nothing is gonna break us apart."

"Right."

Chapter Sixteen:
The Secret's Out

The past few days have been good between Mario and I. We went to the doctor together and got everything squared away. We left the doctor's and went shopping at PG Plaza Mall. We had to find an outfit to wear to this function for Mario's occupation. They were having some type of Players' Ball for all the dealers and their girlfriends or whatever girl they had brought with them.

Mario had given me a wad of cash and told me to find something white to wear to match his Armani suit that he already had. I went into Olive Ole because I saw a white outfit I liked displayed in the window. They had my size and I grabbed it because it was the only one left. I tried it on and it looked great. Now, I just had to find some shoes. I decided on some stilettos I had seen that were about five inches high and had a clear bottom. Mario was gonna love them.

I left there and went to the jewelry counter. I was just browsing when I bumped somebody.

"Oh, excuse me," I said. The guy turned around and it was Jay.

"Yeah, you better excuse yourself," he said smiling. Not sure if he was joking or serious. Didn't matter to me, honestly. "What you doing up here?"

"Shopping, Jermaine."

"Oh. So it's Jermaine now? What happened to Daddy?"

"I have a new man to call Daddy now. Thank you."

"Oh yeah? Does your Daddy know that he can never fill my shoes?"

"That's good. I don't want him to," I said pulling out my phone. I had just received a text from Mario asking where I was. I texted back and told him I was in the food court. I tried to walk away from Jay but he was following me. "Is there something that you want, Jay?"

"Yeah. I wanted you to know I got that problem taken care of."

"That's good. I'm glad you did."

"Now we can hook up like old times."

"Not a chance." I spotted Mario looking around for me. I was trying to shake Jay's ass but it wasn't working. I just headed to where Mario was.

"Hey Mario, look who I ran into?"

"What's up, Cuz?" he said trying to dap Jay up.

"What's up? Y'all two up here together, blood?"

"Yeah, well you know we hanging out."

"You hanging out with my girl?"

"Your girl. Naw, she moved on."

"Moved on to who?"

"Me," he said pulling me by the hand over to him.

Jay shook his head. I could see the anger forming in his face. He turned like he was about to walk away then spun back around and threw a right hook at Mario. He was fast but not fast enough.

Like a cat with instincts, Mario blocked the blow and pushed me out of the way. He charged at Jay and knocked him into some tables. He was on top of him delivering blow after blow. I just stood there, a little shook. I noticed the security people coming and there was no doubt that that were calling the higher authorities.

"Mario, Babe, come on. They're calling the police," I said pulling him by the shirt, trying to get him off Jay. It didn't really help any. He beat on Jay some more before standing over top of him. He looked down at Jay and spat right on him. He grabbed my hand and we ran out of the mall to the parking lot.

Jay was left on the floor of the food court, barely moving. Mario had really put a hurting on him. In a way, Jay deserved it. Maybe not to that extent but deserved it nonetheless. Mario was driving like a damn bat out of hell the whole time.

"Mario, slow down. Please. You're gonna kill us."

He slowed down to the speed limit of 45. "I'm sorry you had to see me act like that, Desi. I just really care about you and it's my job to protect you. I don't give a fuck if that's my cousin or not, you my woman."

I didn't say anything. I just grabbed his hand and kissed his knuckles. This is how someone who loved you treated you. I could say that I love him, all day long, but deep down, my body said something different. My heart belonged to Mario but my soul was owned by my sexual cravings.

****

The night had finally come for us to show out. I hadn't even shown Mario my outfit because of what had gone down. But I knew he was gonna love it.

"Boo, hurry up. I'm almost ready."

"I'm coming," I said from the top of the stairs. I descended to the bottom of the staircase and he looked at me. He had his mouth dropped open. "Close your mouth before the flies get in," I said, laughing as I picked his chin up.

"Damn, Baby you look fucking amazing."

"And so do you."

"Turn around for me. Let me see what my queen working with."

I turned around and I just knew he was lusting. My dress looked great and my stilettos just put the icing on the cake. I looked good, I felt good, and the same went for my man.

"Baby, I swear. You make me wanna fuck you right now."

"I hope you don't think I specifically picked out this dress for nothing."

"What you mean?"

"Easy access."

"How so?"

"I ain't wearing panties. I'm just waiting for you to come get under my dress."

"I don't wanna mess up your dress."

"Suit yourself," I said walking away. My ass was bouncing and I knew he saw it. He pulled me back over to him.

"Just let me get a taste."

"Sure."

He walked me over to the staircase. "Put your foot on the step." I did just that and he got up under my dress and starting playing with my pussy. I gyrated on his lips and quickly came. My sweet nectar dripped down my leg as well as his lips. He got up from the floor and wiped off his suit. "Clean up and we can go."

"Be back in five." I went to the bathroom and washed my pussy and sprayed a little body spray down there. I had come back to the foyer and Mario had two boxes.

"These are for you."

I opened the first box and it was a diamond necklace and earring set. I gasped. "Mario, these are beautiful. Thank you."

"Don't thank me yet. You have another box to open." I grabbed the other one and opened it. A diamond tennis bracelet to match. I started to cry. "Baby, don't cry. You're gonna ruin your makeup."

"I'm sorry," I said dapping at the corners of my eyes. "I just really love these. I love you."

"I love you too. That's why I bought you these gifts. You deserve them."

I looked at him. If only he knew what dark secrets I kept.

We walked out the house and it was a limousine out front. We got in and it was relaxing. I had never been in a limo before. I was acting like a big kid asking Mario what button did what and sipping on champagne. I was getting a little buzzed. And I was getting horny.

We pulled up to The Players' Ball and stepped out onto the red carpet. I felt like a damn celebrity with all of these people snapping pictures of Mario and I. I held onto his arm and we walked down the red carpet like we owned it. In my mind, I did. We looked damn good in our all-white ensembles. They couldn't touch us.

We walked in and Mario introduced me to every hustler and baller and drug dealer. I even saw some community people like cops and lawyers there. It figures. They must be giving them a greater salary than the government for them to risk being here. I had fun mixing and mingling with everybody. It was one of the greatest nights of my life.

There was one guy in particular that kept looking at me. He looked familiar but I couldn't place my finger on it. Where did I know him from? I kept thinking to myself. For the life of me, I couldn't figure it out. I was gonna figure it out eventually, I guess. But right now, I had to use the bathroom and I wanted to freshen up my makeup. I excused myself and headed that way. I looked towards where Mr. Familiar was and I didn't see him anymore.

The bathroom was surprisingly quiet. Two women were leaving when I was walking in. I was freshening up my makeup then I paused. I looked at the person looking back at me. She was beautiful on the outside and ugly on the inside. Because of the way she treated people and used them for sexual pleasures. How could one stop? Was it curable? Could I quit cold turkey? I guess I could but then I would be missing out. I finished my makeup and left the bathroom. I was walking down the hall when someone covered my mouth and snatched me into the coat check room.

"What the fuck?" I yelled, when they uncovered my mouth.

"Shhh calm down," he said. It was the guy from the inside.

"I've been looking at you all night. Don't I know you?"

"You can get to know me. If you know what I mean," he said walking towards me.

"You know my boyfriend is in the other room?"

"Yeah, he is. But you're right here with me."

"Well, you got a point there."

"So what we gonna do?"

I didn't say anything. I just went deeper into the darkness of the coat check room, pulling him by his tie. He kissed me and groped my ass as I wrapped his tie around my hand so he couldn't move. He picked me up and I held my dress up with my hands. He was still kissing me and dry humping my panty- less pussy. His dick was hard. My pussy was wet. He unzipped his pants and pulled his dick out. In an instant, he was inside of my pussy. I held onto his shoulders as he fucked me up against the wall. I didn't even remember telling him to put a condom on. We got so caught up. Oh well. It was too late now. He bounced me on his dick until I came. After I finished, he placed me back on the floor. My legs felt like jelly.

"You didn't even come, um, what's your name?"

"Tim."

"Well, why didn't you come for me, Tim?"

"Don't come in females unless I'm strapped."

"I understand that but you need to get pleasured too," I said, walking close to him. I brushed my breast on him and he gulped.

"It's cool. That was pleasure enough. I been watching you all night long."

"Same here," I said backing him into a corner. "You're gonna bust a nut whether you like it or not." I dropped to my knees and deep throated his still stiff penis. I stroked and sucked and moaned. He moaned and moaned. Sounded like he was trying to get loud but knew he couldn't. Ten minutes, later he shot his kids all in my mouth. And I swallowed it all.

"Your boyfriend is a lucky man."

"I know," I said straightening my clothes and heading towards the door.

"Hold on. Wait," he said walking fast behind me. He handed me a business card. "Call me."

We walked out the coat room seconds apart. Mario was coming towards us. He stopped both of us and looked back and forth between us. "Hey, Baby, I was looking for you."

"Well, here I am. You ready to go?"

"Yep. I'm ready to get you home and in the bed. I been drinking and I need to get up in you."

"Say no more."

We headed towards the exit and our limousine was waiting right there. We hopped in and he told the driver to take the long way home before rolling up the privacy window.

"Why the long way, Mario?"

"I wanted us to enjoy the scenery."

"I wanna enjoy you."

"That's why we going home."

"I want you now," I said throwing my leg across his lap and I sat right on his dick.

"We can wait until we get home. I wanna make love to you."

"No. I want you to fuck me," I said biting his bottom lip.

"You got it." He moved me off his lap and bent me over. He pulled his dick out and rammed it in my pussy. Thankfully it was already wet. He fucked me hard and rough. I thought I was gonna pass out. He fucked me the entire way to the house in different positions. By the time we got home, I was beat. I just went upstairs and took off my dress. I got in the bed ass naked and fell asleep.

Chapter Seventeen:
I Do But I Don't

Mario and I have been with one another for a while now. It's been such a relief not to be hiding it anymore. Especially from Jay. He tolerated it but his ass was still salty about the situation. Nobody cared though. I was downstairs in the kitchen making breakfast when Mario came in.

"Morning, Boo," he said kissing me on the cheek.

"Morning, Baby. Hey, what time did you come in last night?"

"Around like 2. Why?"

"Just asking, Hun. Just making sure you got in safe since you only answer my texts when you want," I responded with a hence of an attitude.

"Sorry, Boo. I will be sure to check in more often."

"Thank you."

"What's for breakfast, love?"

"Your favorite Cinnamon French toast, eggs, sausage, and bacon, with a side of orange juice."

"Oh damn," he said rubbing his hands together as I sat the plate down in front of him. I went to get my plate and I could feel his eyes on me. I turned and caught him.

"What's wrong, Mario?"

"Oh, nothing, Baby. I was just looking at you and you getting a little thick. Daddy like that."

"That I'm getting fat?"

"Oh trust, baby girl, you ain't fat. But that ass is spreading. Daddy's been putting in work."

"Yeah, he has," I said. You have no idea what other daddy is putting in work. I said in my head. I sat down and ate with Mario. I was about to eat a sausage when I jumped up and ran to the bathroom. I threw up a little on the floor but the majority went into the toilet. I could hear Mario running down the hall to the bathroom.

"Are you okay, Boo?"

"Yes," I said still leaning over the toilet seat.

"Is there something you wanna tell me, Desiree?"

"No, Bae."

"Let me ask you something. When was the last time you had your period?"

"Not that long ago," I lied. I haven't had a period in three months; ever since we first started having sex. I thought it was because of stress nonetheless. That's why I haven't said anything.

"Oh ok. Just checking."

I put on my agenda to take a pregnancy test. Like yesterday. I just think it's stress honestly. I finished eating then went upstairs to get ready for my day. I took a quick shower and got dressed. I needed to go get a ginger ale first and foremost. I probably just had a little stomach bug. Yeah, that's it. Mario came into the room just as I was leaving..

"You know I love you right, Desiree?"

"Of course. And I love you too." He kissed me and gave me a hug and told me to have a good day. I told him the same. I took the Range Rover while he drove the Cadillac today. I called Jessica as soon as I got in the car.

'Hey girlie, what you doing?"

"Girl, nothing. Trying to get out the house."

"Well, good. I need you to run an errand with me while Mario is out the house."

"No problem. What kind of errand is it?"

"Not the kind you're thinking, girl," I said, laughing. She always thought I was about to smash somebody. But most of the time she was right though. "I hope you're ready."

"Honey, I was born ready."

"Good. Bring your ass outside," I said before hanging up. Within minutes, Jessica was downstairs and in the whip.

"So what's all this about, Desi?"

"Well, I think I may be pregnant."

"Really? That's good. Why don't you sound excited?"

"I am excited but what if he don't be?"

"He will be."

"I hope you're right."

Jessica and I went to the store and got back in record time. Good thing Mario was gone and would probably be all day. I went into the bathroom to take the test.

"You need me to help you?"

"No, Jess. I got it," I said sitting on the toilet. I pulled the plastic tool out the box and peed on the end. I wiped myself and sat it on the sink.

"Well, what did it say?"

"Nothing yet. It says a few minutes. So while we play the waiting game, I'm gonna go get me a soda."

Nymphopervtress

"Me too."

We went to get sodas and talked for a few minutes before heading back upstairs. We got back to the bathroom and I was so nervous to look at it. I had Jessica do it.

"What does it say?" I asked her.

"Do you want a boy or a girl?"

"What?"

"Yep. Congratulations."

I snatched the test out of her hand and read it for myself. Two lines meant I was pregnant. I'm gonna be a mom. My eyes started to water.

"Those better be happy tears. Right?"

"Yes. I just need a minute."

"When are you gonna tell Mario?"

"I don't know."

"Don't take too long, sweetie."

"I'm not."

"Well, you handle that and I will see you later."

"You don't need me to take you home?"

"Naw, my friend Damien is picking me up from here."

"Oh ok. Tell him I said hello."

"Okay. You take care of yourself and call me if you need anything," she said giving me a hug and a kiss on my cheek. When I heard the door close, I laid back on the bed and started thinking. I was sleep within an hour.

****

I heard the door slam and I jumped up. Oh shit. Its Mario. I hurried to go in the bathroom and wrap up the test. I stuffed it down in the trash can. He would think it was a tampon. As least that's what I was hoping. I went back into the room and laid back. I played possum when I heard him reach the top of the stairs. He clicked on the light. I could feel him standing over me and watching me sleep.

"Hey, Baby, I'm home."

I turned over and rubbed my eyes playing the part. "Hey, Boo," I said, fake-stretching.

"How're you feeling?"

"I feel a little better. I drank a ginger ale and been sleeping all day."

"I'm glad you got some rest. Are you hungry? I got your favorite," he said sitting a tray of food on the bed. I opened it and it was a cheeseburger with fried onions. Just how I liked it.

"I wasn't but now I am," I said, laughing.

"Cool. Imma go wash my hands. You need to brush your teeth because your breath smells like ass."

"Yeah, I was dreaming I was eating yours."

"And your ass had better keep dreaming."

I laughed. I thought he was a freak but not even. He kept saying that he don't think he would like it. I know he would. The guys in the pornos liked it. But then again, they are actors. He came back in there with me and turned on Rush Hour. I needed a movie date like this. Something to take me outta my funk. We ate good carryout and watched a good movie. I was loving every minute of it. When we finished, we laid down and cuddled. I fell asleep in his arms. My safe haven.

"Wake up, Desiree," Mario said, shaking me.

"What's wrong, Bae?" I said groggily.

"What is this?"

I opened my eyes. The test. He must have been snooping in the trash. Damn. "It looks like a pregnancy test, Mario."

"That's exactly what it is. Who's test is it, Desiree?"

"It's mine Mario," I said, in a low tone.

"Why you didn't tell me, Boo? I thought we weren't keeping secrets anymore?"

"I wasn't keeping it a secret. I wanted to surprise you," I lied. Truth was, I wasn't sure if I was gonna keep it or not. Hell, I didn't even know who the damn baby father was. That's the only thing that made matters worse.

"I'm so happy, Babe," he said hugging me. "I'm gonna be a daddy." He was smiling hard as he rubbed on my stomach and made baby talk with my little embryo.

"I'm happy, too," I said. Deep down, I was hurting and breaking into pieces. On the outside, I was smiling and crying right along with him.

"I got something for you, Desi," he said getting up off the bed.

"What is it?"

"Just wait. Close your eyes." I closed my eyes and held out my hands. I figured it was a gift, so why not? "Open your eyes," he said. I opened my eyes and I was shocked. He was down on one knee with a box in his hand that was housing an eight carat princess-cut diamond. My heart stopped for a few seconds and my eyes looked like they were about to pop out of my head. "Desiree Michelle Logan, I love you. I love you even more now that you will be having our child. I was gonna wait to propose to you on Thanksgiving but this seemed way better. I would be honored if you would be my wife."

I just sat there star struck. "I-I-. Yes Mario. I will marry you," I said. I quickly slipped the ring onto my finger. He pulled me off the bed and hugged me tight. "I love you so much. You have made me feel like the luckiest man in the world."

I held onto him and stared at the ring. How could I do this to him? To us? I can't settle down. I loved having sex too much. With Mario as well as others too. What have I just gotten myself into?

Chapter Eighteen:
Wake Me From This Nightmare

I woke up feeling like shit. The previous night was full of endless surprises. Mario proposing was the biggest surprise. I thought it was a joke until he pulled out that rock. How could I say yes when I knew I wanted to still sleep with other people? Would I still be able to do that? I mean, I haven't gotten caught by Mario yet. Maybe I never will. I want to continue doing it but I wouldn't mind being a wife too.

I was sitting in the living room when my phone rang. It was Jessica.

"Hey, girlie," I said after answering.

"Congratulations, Bestie. I saw your post on Facebook. You're gonna be the next Mrs. Hold up, what is Mario's last name?"

"Davis."

"Desiree Davis. Double D. I think it has a nice ring to it."

"I'm sure it does, but I don't think I'm ready."

"Excuse me? What do you mean? You snagged one of the most infamous drug dealers in the game from the East Coast and you talking about 'you don't think you're ready?'"

"Yep."

"Bitch, have you lost your mind?" she asked, yelling into the phone.

"No, I haven't. You know how I am."

"Yeah, but that could stop. But only if you want it to stop."

"I don't."

"Then I don't know what to say. What are you thinking about doing?"

"Well, right now I'm on Tagged, looking for some P.P."

"What the hell is P.P.?"

"Potential Penis," I said, laughing.

"Oh ok. All I'm gonna say is just be careful, honey. You know you can't be wilding like usual since you pregnant now."

"I know. I know. But I just need to get my mind off everything."

"Ok. Call me later."

"Bye." I continued to search through the profiles on Tagged. No one was really catching my eye. I stopped when I saw a guy that was less than ten miles from me. Bingo. I inboxed him and he replied back real quick. His name was KingDingaling.

Me: hey, how are you doing?

KingDingaling: what's up with you, ma?

Me: nothing really. Trynna link up and get some attention for my body.

KingDingaling: oh yeah? What's wrong with your man? He ain't satisfying you right?

Me: he does, but I need more. I'm pregnant and I want somebody to enjoy it since he can't right now.

KingDingaling: pregnant you say? That pussy be fire. I wanna be the lucky guy.

Me: where you wanna meet?

KingDingaling: I can come scoop you.

Me: meet me by Naylor Road Station in ten minutes.

KingDingaling: will do. I will be in a black Ford Focus. VA tags.

Me: cool. I will be in a sundress.

KingDingaling: I'll see you soon.

I went to take a shower and get ready. I looked at myself in the mirror and it looked as if I were glowing. This is usually one of the happiest times in a woman's life but not mine. I would be happy if I knew who's baby it was. I would be happy if I didn't have this problem finding complete satisfaction.

I drove the car down to the metro station and parked in the garage. I sat in the car for a few moments until I saw his Ford Focus pull up. I got out and locked the doors. I walked over to his car and tapped on the window. He rolled the window down and smiled.

"You're even more beautiful in person."

"Thank you," I said smiling.

"You ready to go."

"I thought you'd never ask." I got in the car and we drove off. We drove into an apartment complex that looked abandoned. "Why does this place look like this?"

"Like what?"

"All rundown and deserted."

"It's all in your head. These are just old buildings."

"Oh okay."

We got out the car and went into the building. We walked up two flights of stairs before we reached apartment 201. He unlocked the door and I went in behind him.

"Want something to drink?"

"Yeah, a soda." He went to the kitchen and brought back a soda. I looked around the apartment and it was damn near empty. All except for a sofa, a TV, a TV stand, and a mattress on the floor. "Just moved in?"

"Yeah. I don't have much. Not enough room for it even if I did."

"I see."

"So what you wanna do?"

"Just what I said. I wanna get fucked."

"Then come on."

"Where is your condom?"

"I don't have any. Imma have to run out and get some."

"Naw, it's cool."

"What you mean it's cool?"

"I mean we can fuck without one. It's only one time and I can't wait any longer."

"Bet." He bent me over and lifted up my dress. He rubbed on my pussy and got me wet before entering. He put the swollen head into my tight vagina and I moaned in a sultry voice. "Damn you tight. When was the last time your man been up in here?"

"Last week. That's why I needed it bad."

"And imma make sure you get enough before you leave."

"Okay."

He continued to fuck me slow. Then he grabbed my hands and placed them behind my back as he fucked me harder. I was so into it that I didn't even notice that he had tied my hands up until I tried to move them.

"What's going on?" I asked, trying to sound serious but I was still moaning from his strokes.

"Nothing. I just wanted to try something with you."

"Well, I don't like it so can you let me go?"

"Yeah. Right after you get some more dick."

I guess he must have used some type of code because as soon as he said that, four masked men came from out of nowhere. He pulled out of me and stood up.

"So how is this one?" said the biggest one. He was not that tall but his ass was wider than all outside.

"She official, Boss," KingDingaling said.

"Good job. You finished with her?"

"Naw, B. I wanted to join y'all."

"Cool with me."

"What the fuck is going on?" I yelled at them.

"Aye, G shut that bitch up."

Whoever G was came from behind the chair and slapped me. I instantly broke down crying. "If you just shut your mouth and do what we say, you can walk out of here without an ass whooping or worse. Got it?"

"Yes," I responded sniffling.

The guy who was referred to as Boss came up to me with his pants undone. "Suck my dick, Bitch. And I better like it."

I held back a few tears and maneuvered my head so I could suck his dick. It got hard after a few minutes. I started sucking it slower. Bam! He had hit me with a right hook. "I said do the shit right. I want some bomb-ass-fucking head before I fuck your little ass pussy."

I did as I was told. I closed my eyes and sucked it like it was Mario's. Like it was Jay's. Like it was Scott's. Anybody I could think of, so I could hurry up and get this over with. He pushed me away and pulled my legs so I could be slouched on the couch. He spread my legs apart and put his dick in me. I screamed out in fear. And I screamed out in pleasure. I was petrified right now while my pussy was enjoying this nightmare before my eyes. My body had ultimately betrayed me. While he was fucking me, another fat guy stood over top of me on the sofa. He shoved his dick inside my mouth and had me gagging. He was acting like he wanted me to swallow the entire thing. He was so deep in my throat I could feel the throw up forming. Within minutes, I threw up all over his dick. It didn't stop him though. It seemed like that enticed him even more.

I looked out the corner of my eye and a third guy was coming towards me. He tongue kissed the guy that was fucking me and then began to suck on my nipples. What the fuck kind of freak shit were they doing? Why was I included in this? I saw KingDingaling come up and stand by the action and observe.

"I thought you wanted a piece of this action? Go fuck Double R. I wanna see you fuck him good while he sucks on that hoe's titties."

"Yes sir," he responded before tapping the dude and telling him to bend over. He stuck his dick inside the dude's asshole with such ease. They must do this shit all the time. He grabbed my titty hard as he got fucked.

The last guy, tall and lanky-looking, came over. "Y'all need to switch this bitch around. I wanna get some of that ass." Everybody stopped within seconds to obey his orders. The Boss laid on the floor and sat me down on top of him. The tall guy bent me over and without caution rammed a stiff dry dick right up my ass. I yelped out in pure agony. This nightmare felt like it was going on forever. After a while, I couldn't take it anymore. I let them have their way with my body, unwillingly, and passed out.

I woke up naked in an empty room. There were no lights, no voices and no signs of life. I adjusted my eyes to the darkness and started

Nymphopervtress

to feel around. I was searching for an escape and I found it when I found the door knob. I turned it and reluctantly it opened. I used the light from the hall to find my clothes and phone. I found them and got dressed. I went into the hall and went slowly down the rickety stairs. I noticed blood forming on my pants. How could that be? I can't be on my period while I'm pregnant, I thought to myself. And even if I was, why the hell is so much coming out at once? By the time I had reached the bottom of the stairs, I had doubled over in agonizing pain. I didn't know what was going on. I pulled out my phone and called the police.

Operator: what is the location of the emergency?

Me: I'm not sure where I am. I woke up here. Some guy brought me here.

Operator: what's the problem ma'am?

Me: I was raped. I woke up in an empty apartment and I have blood everywhere.

Operator: are you pregnant, ma'am?

Me: yes.

Operator: okay. I have pinpointed your location. The paramedics and the police will be there shortly.

Me: okay.

I took my shirt off and laid on the dirty floor. I curled up in the fetal position and cried. My cries must have been heard because within moments, the police and paramedics rushed through the door. They put me up on the stretcher just as I was losing consciousness. The last thing I heard was, "I need oxygen. Stat."

****

I woke up again. This time in a bright room with sunlight beaming through my window. Had I died and gone to Heaven? I thought to myself. I adjusted my eyes to the brightness. I was in a hospital room. From wall to wall, all I saw were flowers, teddy bears, cards, and get-well-soon balloons. I didn't see anyone so I buzzed the nurse. Moments later, an elderly nurse came in to assist me.

"Good morning, sunshine. My name is Nurse Nancy. How're you feeling?"

"Like shit."

"I can believe it seeing as how you have been here for the past week."

"Week? How is that possible?"

"You were in a coma, dear."

"A coma?"

"Yes. You were in a bad situation and you were unresponsive for the past week. But I'm sure everyone will be glad to see that you're awake."

"Everyone?"

"Yes. Your family and friends. As well as your fiancé. He must really love you deeply. He has been here every day since you were admitted. He's still here as a matter of fact. Said he wasn't gonna leave until you were discharged."

That sounded just like Mario. Bless his heart. He has spent days by my bedside? That was sweet of him. "Wait. What about my baby?"

"Sorry but you had a miscarriage, honey."

"What?"

"You lost entirely too much blood and we couldn't save the baby."

"Oh my god. Does my fiancé know?"

"Yes, he does. That was the second thought after you. Honey, I'm gonna tell you like this, you have a good man and you better hold onto him. I have never seen a man sit in here for seven days, barely eating or anything. Not these young hell raisers anyway."

That made me laugh a little and it made me choke. My mouth was dry as cotton.

"I will get you some water and let everyone know that you're awake."

"Can you send them in?"

"Will do."

Nurse Nancy left my room and I sat up. It hurt a little but not as bad. I couldn't believe how stupid I had been. Why the fuck didn't I just stay my ass home? I heard a knock at the door. Mario came in, following behind was Shannon, my mom, and my little sister.

"Oh, baby, I'm so glad you're alright," Mario said, rushing over to me.

"How are you feeling?" my little sister asked.

"Like a pile of crap."

"That's what you look like too," she said, with an uneasy smile on her face.

"Thanks a lot sis," I said, with a smile.

"Don't worry, baby girl. We're gonna get those bastards," my mom said angrily. "Nobody hurts my kids and gets away with it."

"That's right," Mario said in agreement. "I already got Rocko out looking for them niggas where the ambulance picked you up from. And when I find them, it's gonna be a wrap."

I looked at my mother and she just nodded her head. "Let him take care of things, Desi. No telling how many times this shit has happened before."

"You're right. Thanks, Baby. I love you."

"I love you too."

"I'm sorry, Baby," I said, starting to cry.

"Sorry for what?"

"For all of this. Especially for losing the baby."

"Don't you blame yourself for that. None of this shit was your fault, Boo."

Deep down, it really was my fault but he thought I was just saying that. I was feeling really bad for all of this shit. I was gonna be miserable. I have gotten raped. I have lost my first child. What's next?

"I wanna get some rest, Baby," I said, scooting back down in the bed.

"Okay. I'm not going anywhere but I'm gonna walk your folks out to their car."

"Okay, Hun." My mom and sister came over and gave me a hug and kiss. They both told me to get better soon. As they walked out, Nurse Nancy was coming back with my water and a tray of food. When I caught a whiff of the meal, my stomach instantly started growling. Guess I should eat something before laying back down. She moved the table over to my bedside. I ate the food until I thought I had eaten enough. I washed it down with my orange juice and a couple sips of water. I laid back down and instantly fell back to sleep.

****

"Wake up, Baby," I heard Mario say, as he shook me from my slumber. I opened my eyes to see Mario and a detective at my bedside.

"What's going on, Mario?" I asked, awaking fully and sitting up.

"This is Detective Marshall. He is gonna be handling your case and wanted to ask you some questions."

"Okay," I said uneasily.

"How are you doing, Ms. Logan?"

"Well, with all that has happened I'm glad I'm alive. I'm just sorry I lost my baby."

"Yes, you were pregnant. And I'm so sorry for your loss. For the record, do you know how far along you were?"

I thought about it. "No, I didn't."

Well, judging from what the nurse told me about your last menstrual, you were about five months."

"Sure. I guess so." I looked over at Mario who had his head hung low like he had just been defeated.

"Can you tell me about the incident in question?"

"What do you wanna know?"

"Anything that you can remember about when you were raped."

I took a long pause to think. I couldn't tell the truth so I quickly made up a lie. "Well, I was walking around at the mall. I was walking to where I had parked and I heard somebody yell something down the street. As soon as I turned to look and see where the voice was coming from, somebody pulled me up in a van that I was standing by. They were all masked so I can't identify them. They took me to where you all found me at. They took turns fucking me and making me give them head. They were slapping me and punching me. Eventually I passed out and when I woke up, they were gone." I stopped talking and he was still writing.

"Was that it?"

"No. I called the police and they, as well as the paramedics came but I was unconscious when they arrived."

"Anything else?"

"No."

"Well, thanks. If I have any further questions I will be contacting you or your fiancé."

"Okay."

"You take care and get better."

"Thanks." Detective Marshall left the room and Mario closed the door. He walked back over to where I was and sat in the chair by my bed.

"I can't believe you were five months pregnant, Babe. I think we would have been great parents."

"I know Boo, but we can always try again."

"Seriously?"

"Yes, Mario. I would want nothing more than to have your baby."

"I'm so glad to hear you say that," he said, standing up and hugging me.

Truth be told, I am happy and sad about losing my baby. But at least I would never have to second guess who the father was. At least the next time, I will know its Mario's baby. At least I hoped so.

Chapter Nineteen:
My Besties

It's been an entire three days since I had been discharged from the hospital. Mario has been waiting on me hand and foot. I liked it the first day and a half but now it was getting annoying. I needed him away from me so I could try to do things for myself.

"I'm gonna go get me something to drink. Do you want anything?"

"Baby, I got it."

"Look Mario, I know you mean well but I have to get up and do shit myself, okay?"

"But, Babe, I'm your man. The man that you're gonna marry. I'm gonna be there for you through sickness and in health. So therefore I'm supposed to take care of you."

I chuckled a little bit. "Since you put it like that, this is my theory. We both will say those vows but at the end of the day, we're a team. If you don't wanna be a team then be solo," I said folding my arms across my chest.

"Okay, you win. We will both go and get ourselves a drink. Is that okay with you, Boss?"

"Yes it is." We walked to the kitchen and got a soda. My phone had rang and I looked at the caller id. It was Jessica.

"Hey girl, what's up?"

"Nothing really. How are you doing?"

"I'm good. Just a little upset that my best friend has been avoiding me. What's up with that, Jess?"

"I'm sorry. I don't know. It's just that I was scared and was thinking the worst."

"Well, I'm fine. So can I come see my best friend?"

"Aren't you supposed to be on bed rest, Desi?"

"Yeah, but I'm fine. Mario has nursed me back to health, so I'm good. How about I come over for the weekend?"

"That's cool with me."

"Cool. I will see you tomorrow evening."

"Okay, girl." I hung up the phone and I noticed Mario staring at me, laughing and shaking his head.

"What?"

"You're so hardheaded. But you have fun with your girl this weekend."

"Thanks, Babe," I said, giving him a hug. "I really do feel better. No more bruises on my body, I stopped bleeding, and thanks to you, my body probably has gotten the best healthy diet in history," I said, laughing.

"Well, since you feeling that good, how about we go upstairs?"

"To do what?"

"Workout a little."

"How about we try to work on our legacy?"

"That sounds even better." He scooped me up in his arms and took me to our bedroom. He made sweet love to me like never before. I was enjoying it but I was missing something. I wanted to be fucked but he wanted to make love. Since I wasn't gonna get what I wanted from him, I knew where I could get it from. We finished our lovemaking session and I went to sleep.

****

The next day was already starting off great. It was the end of October and it was still a little hot out. This was a little odd, but hey, I didn't create Mother Nature. I decided on wearing some skinny jeans and my new balance sneakers with a plain top today. I pulled my hair back into a slick ponytail and observed.

"Damn, you looking good girl," I said to my reflection. "Even though you have been through this whole ordeal, it will get better." I always had a thing about talking to myself to lift myself up. To make myself feel better. I wasn't used to people doing that for me except Mario.

I don't understand how I managed to keep Mario around this long. He was handsome, charming, and could hustle his ass off. One of the most infamous dealers that had ever walked the streets of the nation's capital, and I sleep next to him every night. I loved him and everything he did but I still lusted after others. I would actually get mad at him if I caught him staring at other females. And he would always say, "Babe don't trip. I'm just looking. It's not a crime to look. I just won't touch." I wish I followed that motto. Instead I would look, touch, suck, and fuck. Then I wouldn't have any remorse for what I had done. I wasn't a good girl at all but in Mario's eyes, I was a queen. And his ass worshiped the ground that I walked on.

I jogged down the steps and Mario was on the couch watching the news. I never watched the news because it was always something sad being said that would have me thinking about it all day. Sometimes I didn't even wanna login to my Facebook account because they would have it on there as well. I

Nymphopervtress

walked up behind him and kissed him on the cheek. "Morning, Bae."

"Good morning to you, Shorty," he said, turning and watching me go into the kitchen. "You look good and full of energy today. How're you feeling?"

I walked back to the living room with two bottles of water. I handed him one and sat down on the sofa and threw my feet across his lap. "I feel great, Mario. The sun is shining. I'm not having any pain. I'm good."

"And why is that?"

"It's because of you, Mario. You know I'm still a little upset about losing the baby, but hey, I thought it out and maybe it just wasn't time. Every situation happens for a reason."

"That's right," he nodded his head in agreement.

"And now we can work on creating our baby again."

"How about right now?"

"Nope. I just thought of some things I wanted to do with you today."

"Does it involve us getting naked and being wrapped in sheets?" he asked, smiling.

"No, you freak," I said, laughing. "Just come with me."

"You lucky I'm already dressed. If I wasn't, I would've tempted you with my body."

"I know. That's why I'm glad you have clothes on too."

We left the house and we drove to Ihop. "What are we doing here?"

"You're gonna see." In the back of my mind, I hoped today was gonna be perfect. It was Mario's 26th birthday and I think he suspects that I forgot. We walked into Ihop and we were instantly escorted to a table that I was actually able to reserve just for us.

"What's going on, Desi?"

"I just wanted to take you out and spend the day with you for your birthday." He looked at me with a shocked look. "Yes, your birthday. I didn't forget about it," I said, laughing and smiling.

"I thought you did, honestly. I ain't get a birthday kiss or nothing."

"Would you like one now?"

"Hell yeah I would." I got up and went over to his side of the table. I kissed him and he kissed me back. We were so deep in our kiss we didn't even know the waitress came until she cleared her throat. We broke away from our kiss and she sat our food down. I had already told them what I wanted us to have. French toast, scrambled eggs, turkey bacon, and a birthday candle for his. We ate good and enjoyed our little date.

"Now that I'm full, what's next?"

"Stop asking questions and just enjoy it. Please and thank you."

"Yes ma'am, Miss Lady."

Next on my list was shopping. But first I had a little gift for him. "Open this," I said, pulling a bag from the backseat.

"Aww, Boo, you shouldn't have," he said jokingly. He took out the tissue paper and laid his eyes on his gifts. A Polo Red cologne gift set, a Polo wallet, and two tickets to tonight's Miami Heat vs Washington Wizards game. "Oh my god, Boo. You must have known I really wanted to go to that game. And they are floor seats!" he said, with his eyes popping out his head. I couldn't do nothing but smile and cheese hard, right along with him.

"I did, and you deserve it, Babe. After all you have done for me in the past seven months, I just wanted to show my appreciation."

"But Babe, how could you afford these tickets?"

"I've been saving some of the money so I could make sure your birthday was special."

"I love you so much." He pulled me close to him and hugged me tight.

"I love you too." Now onto our next stop. We were heading to the mall so my man could get something to wear for tonight. He had to look good whether I was on his arm or not.

"I just thought of something."

"What's that?" I asked.

"You gave me two tickets for the game. And I know the other one doesn't belong to you. Does it?"

"Oh no, Poppy. Those tickets are for you and Jay."

"Jay?"

"Yeah. I thought since y'all are actually back speaking and on good terms, y'all could go together."

"True. Does he know about the tickets?"

"Nope."

"I'm about to call him."

"Well, you do that and I will go find you something."

"Cool."

I walked into the Last Stop store. I found him a pair of jeans that he could wear, with his Jordans that I had gotten from a shoe connect. I found a purple and black Jordan shirt to wear with them as well. I went across to the jewelry store. I looked over all the lovely pieces until I laid my eyes on a diamond cross. I asked to see it and the little guy behind the counter opened the case. I lifted it from its bed and it wasn't as heavy or as big as it looked. The chain was long enough for his tall ass too. I dropped three stacks on it and left.

I did all of this within one hour. If he were with me bugging me, we would still be shopping. Speaking of Mario, where was he?

I walked into all the stores and I couldn't find him. I decided to go check the parking lot where we had parked. He was standing outside the car on the phone. I walked over to where he was and he smiled. "Aight, son. Imma see you later on." He hung up the phone.

"You were talking to Jay that whole time?"

"Yep, and he said thanks for getting him a ticket to the game. I really appreciate everything that you have done for me today. No woman has ever done anything for me. Well, except my mom but she doesn't really count."

"Well, don't thank me yet. Everything I planned for today isn't done."

"Really? What did you get me to wear tonight?" I handed him the bag with the clothes in it. "Cool. Cool."

"I have one more thing." I handed him the jewelry bag and he opened the box that was inside.

"Oh shit, Boo." He put the chain around his neck. "It's perfect. I love it."

"I'm glad," I said, walking around to the trunk. "This is your last gift." He walked around to the back of the truck with me and I opened his shoe box.

"The new Js, Boo? Oh my god! You made a nigga feel good today," he responded hugging me and rocking back and forth. "If you ain't have them pants on, I would fuck you right now."

"And what's holding you back?"

"Other than them jeans, not a damn thing."

I looked around and I didn't see anybody close to the end where we were. I sat inside the truck and removed my shoes and my pants. "What are you doing?"

"I'm giving you what you want, Daddy."

"You're crazy."

"Yeah, about you. Now are you gonna stand there and keep rapping, or are you gonna hop in the truck and get some of your pussy?" I asked, bending over the back seat.

"Shit, you ain't gotta ask me twice." He did the same as I did and closed the door to the back of the truck. He stuck his dick inside me and fucked me right in the back of the truck. The truck was rocking and we were laughing at the people that were walking by and noticing it. Luckily, they couldn't see us because of the pitch black tint. As soon as we finished, we noticed a police car heading our way. We jumped into our seats and sped off. No need to get into trouble for pleasing my man. We laughed as we drove off and saw the police car in our rearview. He stopped at the end of the block and we kept going.

****

It was finally time to ditch Mario for the weekend. He was going out with his cousin and I was gonna be chilling with my best friend. I had showered and changed my clothes. Jessica had called and said Shannon wanted to go out to grab a bite to eat. I decided against it and said we should all order in. Mario had just finished spraying on cologne when I walked out the bathroom.

"Damn, pulling out the new cologne already?" I asked, smacking his butt.

"Yeah, I gotta represent. My boo hooked me up from head to toe so I had to top it off with the cologne you had bought me for my birthday too."

"You better. And don't let those little hoes be sniffing around you either."

"Oh yeah? What about if they wanna give me some head? You know as soon as they see the print, they gonna wanna test it out."

"Oh really?" I said, turning him around and dropping to my knees. I pulled his dick out through his zipper and started sucking his dark chocolate meat. I sucked it and deep-throated it. I haven't given him any oral pleasure since the incident happened. I had a flashback and I opened my eyes. Only to realize that it was my man's dick in my mouth. I stopped as soon as I thought he was about to come. I stood up and wiped off my pants and wiped my mouth with the back of my hand.

"Now you think about that when some little whore tries to suck that dick. If I find out, that bitch gonna die."

"Yes, ma'am. I will be on my best behavior. And the same goes for you."

"I know," I said, kissing him on the cheek. I grabbed my backpack and we both headed down the steps. He grabbed the car keys and I grabbed the keys to the truck.

"Y'all better not mess up my truck."

"We already did that earlier, remember?"

"Yes, I do," he said, rubbing his groin on my butt. "I wish we could do it again right now."

"Next time, Boo."

"Okay." He walked me to the truck and helped me in. "Be careful."

"You too." We kissed and I quickly started the car and pulled off. I couldn't wait to get to Jessica's house. I missed her.

I pulled up and saw that Shannon was already there. I also saw that Jessica's dad was there, too. Maybe I can get some dick from him tonight. I thought to myself. We hadn't had sex in a while and I wouldn't mind some now. I walked up to the door and knocked. Jessica's dad opened the door.

"Hey, Mr. Cooper."

"Hey, Desiree. The girls are in Jessica's room," he said, stepping aside.

"Okay." I touched his limp penis and he pinched my ass as I walked by. He wanted me. I walked to Jessica's room and I heard the music playing.

"Hey bitches," I said as I walked into her room.

"What's up, girl?" Shannon said as she gave me a hug.

"I missed you guys."

"We missed you too," Jessica said, hugging me.

"What are you broads in here doing?"

"Well, nothing really. I don't know why y'all always wanna come to my house. My house is boring," Jessica said.

"We can watch movies."

"Yeah. Let's watch The Texas Chainsaw Massacre."

"What is it with you and all these damn horror movies? Do you plan on snapping out from sanity one day or something?" Shannon asked.

I threw my head back in laughter. "No, girl. I just love all the gore."

"I bet. But let's watch it. Trey Songz died stupid in that movie."

"Yeah, I wanted to see that monster fuck him up," Jessica chimed in.

"I know right."

We sat and chilled and watched movies. It was fun to be around the girls again. I didn't know what to do with myself all this time. But I'm glad my life is getting back to normal. Shannon and Jessica fell asleep so I decided to sneak out and check on Mr. Cooper.

I tapped at the door before entering. "Hey, Mr. Cooper."

"Hey. Are the girls asleep?"

"Yes."

"Good. I have been missing that mouth of yours," he said, taking off his boxers. He must have been horny because his penis was already sticking up. He came over to me and pushed me down to my knees. He forced his dick in my mouth and fucked my face. He came fairly quickly and I know at his age, it wasn't getting back up no time soon. So, I cleaned up my mouth and went back to Jessica's room. I laid down a little frustrated and dozed off to sleep.

My pussy was wet. In my dream, I had been having sex with five dudes. Kind of like the incident that happened to me. But for some reason it turned me on. Maybe I wasn't raped. I was just a part of a gangbang. Whatever it was, I needed to get it again since I was thinking about it. I was turning in my sleep and it felt as though I was being held down. I woke up and I noticed somebody between my legs. I thought it was Jessica's dad so I grabbed my phone and used its light. I turned the flashlight on only to find that Jessica was eating my kitty.

She put a finger to her lips to tell me to keep quiet. "What the hell is going on?" I whispered to her.

"I just wanna have fun," Jessica whispered back. I watched as she planted sweet kisses on my vagina. She fingered my pussy as she licked my clit. This felt a little better coming from her than it did from Mario. But I didn't get it. I thought Shannon was the lesbian? Maybe they both were. I didn't care. I just wanted to enjoy the head I was receiving. I have never been with a girl sexually other than what happened between Shannon and me. This could be fun.

"Oohh," I lightly moaned. I was grabbing her hair and thrusting my pussy into her face. She started eating faster. I was so caught up I didn't even notice that Shannon had woke up.

"What's going on?" she asked, rubbing her eyes.

"You wanna join?"

"Hell yeah," she said. She moved up behind Jessica and spread her ass cheeks. She stuck her tongue and licked up and down her crack. She reached her arms around Jessica and fondled her breasts and I moved Jessica's hands up to play with mine. It was like something right out of a flick. Shannon and Jessica sat up in front of me and kissed. I sucked on Jessica's nipples and played with Shannon's. Then Jessica kissed me and then Shannon and I exchanged spit. I reached in my bag and pulled out Kong. "Lay back, Jess," I said. She laid on her back and I got in front of her. I placed my face down to where her pussy was and it smelled so sweet. I flicked the tip of my tongue across her clit. I liked it and I kept going until I was licking every inch of that pussy. I stuck Kong inside her and sucked on her titties.

All the while, Shannon had reached into her bag and pulled out a strap on. Oh wow. "Suck my dick, Desiree."

"Don't mind if I do," I responded as I crawled over to where she was standing and grabbed ahold of her dildo. I sucked it like it was a real dick.

"Yes, suck my dick, you cunt." Damn and dirty talk? I was really enjoying this. "This is the dick you can get when you with me. You understand me?" she asked, slapping me.

"Yes, Shannon."

"You call me Daddy," she said, slapping me again.

"Yes, Daddy." She took her fake dick out my mouth and pushed me down to where Jessica was.

"I want you to eat her pussy while I fuck you."

"Yes, Daddy."

I dove my face in her crotch again. Shannon rammed that big nine inch dildo right inside my wet pussy. I had come all over it and I had squirt all over the place. "Your turn, Jessica," she said. Jessica bent down between my legs and she got fucked too. She got a spanking and everything. I didn't get that and I wanted that. Within ten minutes, Jessica and Shannon had both come at the same time.

We looked at the clock and it was 3 a.m. We wasn't even tired. By the time 8 a.m. came, we were all spanked, fucked, and squirted out. This was truly a night to remember with my best friends.

Chapter Twenty:
3 Is Not A Crowd

Every day since that incident happened, I had been thinking about that gangbang. It wasn't bad thoughts. It was kind of weird because I wanted to be a part of one now. A planned one though because that was more like an ambush. Then there was the event that happened between me, Shannon, and Jessica. I enjoyed my night with them but now I wanted to have another night like that—but with dicks. And lots of them.

I was lying next to Mario and touching myself. I guess he felt the motions of the bed because he woke up.

"So you trynna exclude me from the festivities?" he asked, turning on his side to fully face me.

"Not at all, Baby. I was getting her ready before I woke you up," I lied.

"You didn't have to do that, Hun. You know I love to help out."

"Well, it ain't too late, Daddy," I said, moving my hand and spreading my legs wider. He got up and went face first between my thighs. He sucked and licked on my clit. He played with my pussy for a few more minutes and then started fucking me. I reached over and pulled Kong out the night drawer and started sucking him.

"Oohh, you nasty," he exclaimed. He took Kong out of my hand and pushed it in and out of my mouth.

"Play with my ass, baby," I said as I took ahold of Kong. He turned me over onto my knees. He fucked my pussy from behind. I closed my eyes when I felt his finger go into my asshole. I continued to suck on Kong as he fucked both of my holes. Getting penetrated in all three holes felt rejuvenating. It felt like an entire new level of ecstasy. By the time it came for Mario to release his kids, I had beat him to the punch. He hit my spot and it felt like Niagara Falls just gushed out of my body. Even after he had come, I was just starting to leak. Once it stopped, we got up and took the comforter off the bed.

"What was that?" Mario asked me when we got in the shower.

"What was what?" I asked, looking at him dumbfounded.

"All of that, Desiree. I mean, don't get me wrong I enjoyed the fuck out of it, but where did that come from?"

"I just been thinking about some things and watching some flicks and thought it would be nice to try. That's all."

Nymphopervtress

"Well, I don't know what you been watching but keep it up," he said, laughing. We washed and made out in the shower before getting out.

It was noon on a cool November day. It was actually the week of Thanksgiving. I didn't know what we had planned. Nobody talked about anything so I guess I was just gonna sit home and watch the football game like usual. I heard my phone ring. I read the caller id: Mario.

"Really, Mario?"

"What?"

"Why are you calling me from upstairs? You know I never left."

"I know. I just talked with my dad and he wanted to know if you wanted to cook Thanksgiving dinner here. You can invite your mom and Monet. It's about time that your mom met my parents."

I got silent on the phone. I wasn't too sure about that. What if his parents didn't like me? Especially his mom. "Um, sure, that would be great, babe. I will call and let my mother know right now."

"Cool beans."

I hung up the phone smiling. He was such a geek at times saying 'cool beans' like it was cool. It was kind of catchy but I would never admit it. I called my mom. She didn't answer but she sent a text:

Mom: at work

Me: my bad, but Mario wanted to know if y'all wanted to come over for Thanksgiving dinner

Mom: hell yeah, that means I don't have to cook

Me: uh yes, you do you gotta help me

Mom: I guess, Desiree. I will be over there early tomorrow morning so dinner can be ready by 6

Me: okay ma. I will go to the store to get the stuff to cook and we already got a turkey

Mom: okay, sweetie. We will see you in the morning. Love u

Me: love u 2, mommy

I had a great mom and I knew it. I loved her and I couldn't imagine ever a day going by without her calling me or texting me just to check on me and tell me she loves me. I called Mario back but he texted. What the hell was wrong with people today?

Mario: on a business call. Whats up, wifey?

Me: wifey? I like the sound of that

Mario: I bet you do

Me: anyway, mommy said she will be here tomorrow to help me get dinner ready

Mario: cool. What time you going to the store?

Me: I'm gonna leave out in like 30

Mario: what you gonna do in the mean time?

Me: what you want me to be doing?

Mario: bending over for daddy

Me: don't you ever get enough?

Mario: I could never get enough of you, baby

Me: come here

By the time he got downstairs to the living room, I was bent over on the sofa with nothing but my bra and panties on. He walked over and I could see his penis trying to jump out of his jeans. He undid his belt and dropped his pants around his ankles. He got up on the chair behind me and stuck his thick dick inside me. "Aahh," I yelled out. It felt so good. It felt like his arm was inside my pussy versus it being his dick. I threw that pussy at him and he thrusted his dick inside me. He came in fifteen minutes. I cleaned up and left out to head to the store.

As I drove to the store, I still had sex on my mind. I didn't know why. I had sex twice this morning with the man that wants to marry me and I still wasn't satisfied. Is this how it would be for the rest of my life? I didn't know nor did I have an answer to either one of my own questions. Maybe I could have my cake and eat it too. I could marry Mario and get my satisfaction from him and others. Yeah, that could work.

I walked into the store and it was packed with last minute shoppers like myself. I was picking out ingredients and stuff when I saw a really handsome guy working the produce section. My pussy started getting that itch it always got when I was attracted to somebody. I walked over in my sexy walk and pretended like I needed help.

"Excuse me, uh, Derek," I said, reading his name tag. "I need some help getting stuff for salad."

"Well, it looks like you have everything," he said, looking into my shopping cart. "You got salad mix, tomatoes, dressing, cheese and some meats. What else were you looking for?"

"I need a cucumber."

"Well, you just walked past them."

"I saw those and I wasn't impressed. I need a big one. Do you have anymore in the back?"

"Yeah, I do. Give me a sec to go get them."

"Okay." I waited until he went through the double doors and looked around before I headed towards the doors. The coast was clear so I slipped through the doors and looked for him. Nobody was back there so there was no way I was gonna get caught.

He was coming out of the cooler with his back turned. When he turned around and saw me it startled him and he dropped the box of cucumbers. "You scared me," he said, trying to catch his breath.

"Sorry about that. I thought you had forgotten about me."

"No, I didn't. I had to go deep into the cooler to find them."

"Do you like to go deep into stuff, Derek?" I asked, walking closer to him and putting my breasts up in his face.

"Yeah. I mean no. I mean, are we still talking about the cucumbers?"

"Yeah, we are," I said, looking down into the box. I picked up the fattest one that I saw and showed him. "This is perfect."

"Good choice. That is gonna be perfect."

"Would you like to help me again?"

"That's my job. I'm supposed to be customer friendly."

"I like that," I said. "I want you to help me put this cucumber inside my pussy."

"Come again?"

"I said. I want you. To help me. Put that fat cucumber. Inside my tight pussy. Can you do that for me, Derek?"

"Um, sure, I guess," he said nervously.

"Great." I pulled him back into the cooler and closed the door.

"We can freeze to death in here."

"Yeah, if we get locked in, but we're not. That's why they have that button on the door," I said, pointing.

"Okay."

I had on one of those long skirts so I had to hike it up over my waist. After our session earlier, I didn't even bother putting panties back on. I sat on top of a stack of boxes and spread my legs open. "Put it in," I demanded. He walked over and gently placed the cold vegetable on my hot pussy. The coldness made me tingle a little. I spread my pussy lips open and he put inch by inch of the cucumber into my pussy. I rubbed on his dick through his pants as he did that.

"This can't be really happening," he said, as he continued to fuck me with the cucumber.

"It is happening. And you're getting turned on."

"What guy wouldn't? A beautiful girl comes into your job and asks you to fuck her with one of the products in your department. This is like a fantasy come true. I want to fuck you so bad."

"I want you to fuck me too."

"But I don't have a condom."

"I do," I said grabbing my purse and pulling out a condom. He tore the condom open. "Not yet, Derek. I wanna feel the cucumber some more."

"No problem." He put the cucumber back inside me and began to penetrate me again. This time it was going in deeper. It was stretching my pussy out.

"What the hell is going on back here?" said a gruff voice from behind us. We both looked and it was the manager of the store. "What the hell are you doing, Derek?"

"Um, I, um. I don't know, Nathan," Derek said, babbling like an idiot.

"He's tending to a customer. He's helping me. Isn't that in his job description?"

"It is, but this is not. I can fire you for this, Derek."

"Yeah, you could," I said, butting in, "or you can join us," I responded, rubbing on his groin.

"Young lady stop that right now," he said, looking at my pussy.

"Do you really want me to stop, Nathan? I can make you feel good too." I took my shirt off so he could see my perky breasts and my hard nipples.

"No, I don't want you to stop."

"Then stop talking and join in. Don't worry about the cold. You will be hot before you know it." I grabbed his hand and pulled him over to where my head was. I changed my position so that I could lie down now. "Derek put the cucumber back in my pussy and put that condom on. I want you to get up in my ass. Nathan, I want to suck your dick so drop those pants," I ordered both of them. They did what I had told them to do. I caught a glimpse of Derek before he stuck his dick in my ass and it looked just like the cucumber! I felt pain as soon as he put it in and it made me whimper.

"Do you want me to stop?"

"No, keep going. It's painful but it's more pleasurable than anything." He put it back in and kept going. I was crying a little but sucking Nathan's fat cock took my mind off the pain. He reached down and grabbed the cucumber and rammed it in and out of my vagina. Eventually, they changed positions and continued to live out their fantasy. They were enjoying it and so was I. They both had come at the same time and I came moments after. We all cleaned up with some sanitized wipes and fixed our clothes.

"What's your name by the way?" Nathan asked.

"Leslie," I lied, and walked out from the back. I continued to grocery shop like nothing had just taken place. I paid for my groceries and headed home. That was an eventful experience but still wasn't enough. I was gonna keep getting fucked by multiple people until this urge was taken care of. So I texted my besties and told them to meet at my house. I told Jessica to wear a skirt and Shannon to wear sweats and not to forget her dick at home.

****

I pulled up to the house and they were both sitting in Shannon's Altima.

"Hurry up, y'all. Help me get the groceries inside," I said as I popped the trunk.

"What's the rush?" Shannon asked.

"I want us to relieve some stress before Mario gets home."

"Oh ok," Jessica said.

We all grabbed bags and scurried into the house. We put the groceries up with quickness then we ran upstairs to one of the vacant rooms. It was the perfect size bed in this room. It slept six people. As soon as we got in the room, Jessica and I started tongue kissing and fondling each other. Shannon had come up behind me and was kissing on the back of my neck and grabbing on Jessica's ass. I could feel her dick against my butt and I started grinding on it. She grabbed my hips and rubbed it against me some more. We broke from our embrace and went to the bed. Shannon took her time taking off me and Jessica's clothes piece by piece. Every part of our body that was covered in clothing was now exposed for all eyes to see. After we were fully naked, she had us both lay back on the bed as she feasted on our pussies. I guess she was full when she stood straight up. We both knelt on the bed and sucked on her strap on like it was a real dick. It was turning her on seeing both of us pleasure her. She pushed us back on the bed and got on top of Jessica first.

She placed the fake dick inside of Jessica and moved her hips back and forth. I was laying beside her, sucking her titties as Shannon played with my pussy. "Oohh, shit. Fuck!," I moaned and screamed. The door opened and we all stopped. Mario was standing there looking.

Not a sound was made. He looked at all three of us with his mouth sitting open. Without saying a word, he just started stripping out of his clothes. "Continue," was all he said. So we did. Shannon was now squeezing my left breast and Jessica was back to kissing me. Mario got on the bed and got on top of me. He stuck his already hard dick inside me and I shrieked. It felt good to have his dick inside of me.

He and Shannon were just having a good ol' time fucking the shit out of Jessica and me. "Are we gonna change partners, Shannon?" he asked.

"That's up to, Desiree. I don't mind fucking her but I don't know how she feels about you fucking Jess." They all looked at me.

"It's only for this time or when we have sex like this."

"Got you, baby." They swapped spots and Mario put on a condom before sticking his dick inside Jessica. We were still making out and kissing all over each other as we got fucked. When Shannon and Mario were finished, Jessica and I still hadn't come yet. I got on top of her and rubbed my pussy against hers. It was definitely on the list with the top feel good things. We humped each other then played with each other's pussies until we started squirting all over the place. Shannon was there to catch Jessica's and Mario had caught mine. This wasn't a crowd at all. This was like heaven to me.

Chapter Twenty-One:
Disaster At Dinner

❧

Yesterday was just crazy all around. I fucked guys that work at a grocery store and I had an orgy with my fiancé and my two best friends. What more could I ask for? Oh yeah, more sex! Long, hard, rough sex. That's what I want next. I really shouldn't be thinking about that right now. It was family time and we were all enjoying dinner and the football game.

"What is going on between you two?" my mom asked when we went into the kitchen. I wanted to start the dishes as soon as possible.

"Nothing, ma."

"Nothing? You can't tell me it's nothing when you got that big rock on your finger," she said, pointing at my hand.

"Ok, ok. He proposed to me a few months back."

"That's good, baby. I'm so happy for you," she said, hugging me tight. It felt good on the outside but on the inside, I felt like shit. Worse than shit. I felt like scum. But I would never tell her that. Mario had come into the kitchen and caught us hugging.

"What's going on in here?" he asked, walking over to us.

"I just told ma the good news."

"And?"

"And I would have never asked for a better man to be my future son-in-law," she said, hugging him.

"Aww thanks, Ms. Denise."

"Ms. Denise? Boy you better stop calling me that and start calling me ma."

"Well, thanks ma. I really appreciate it."

"No problem. Where is your mom? Does she know?"

"Yeah, she said something to me earlier."

"That's good. Well, she and I need to go talk now. We have a wedding to start planning." She exited the kitchen and left us there.

Everything was going good and everyone was having a good time. Next thing I know, I heard the front door bust open. Two masked guys ran into the house with guns drawn. "Don't nobody move," the first one said. "I want everybody's jewelry, money, everything that's valuable. You too, Mr. Kingpin. Take me to where your stash at." He put the gun into Mario's back

Nymphopervtress

and Mario headed to the basement. The other gunman was left to watch us. He came towards me.

"You must be wifey, huh?" he asked rubbing the barrel of his gun down the side of my face.

"Leave her alone," my mother yelled through her tears.

"Shut the fuck up, Bitch. Now I asked you a question?"

"Yeah, I am."

"I figured. Just by the way you dressed. Let me see what you working with."

"What?" I asked looking at him.

"Take your fucking clothes off, Hoe. Show me what the fuck got this nigga pussy whipped."

I did as I was told and peeled off each piece of clothing. My mother and Mario's mother were sitting there crying. His father was holding his head down in defeat and held onto Monet.

"Yeah, that's it. Let me see that body. Take that bra off. The panties, too." I took my undergarments off and stood there feeling humiliated. I didn't even shed a tear. Mario taught me to fear nothing and never show any sign of weakness. The gunman came over to me and felt me up. He placed his gun on my pelvis and told me to open my legs. "If you move, I'm gonna shoot you right in the pussy." He grabbed me by my hair and pulled my head back. He kissed me on my lips roughly and then dropped me to the floor. I saw him fidgeting with the zipper on his pants until it opened and out came a bumpy penis. It looked like it was written in braille. "Suck my dick, Bitch."

"No," I said scooting back on the kitchen floor.

"You can do it for that nigga but not for me, huh? Get your ass over here." He snatched me from the floor and shoved my face into his groin. His dick was in my mouth and it smelled bad as well as tasted horrible. "That's right. Suck my cock, you whore. And you better not fucking bite me or your brains gonna be painting these walls." My mother screamed a horror movie scream having to sit there and watch this. "Don't rush her, moms, you and those other two bitches are gonna be next. Hell, maybe pops too." I heard a gunshot ring out, followed by footsteps running up the steps. The gunman pushed me away and walked off fixing his clothes. I used this opportunity to grab the gun that Mario kept taped under the table. The gunman came back and walked right into my gun.

"You ain't gonna shoot me, Bitch," he said cockily.

"Yes I am. Or maybe I should let my husband do it."

"That nigga's dead. You heard the gunshot downstairs. My man probably getting some extra stuff to take." The nine millimeter clicked in his ear.

"Or maybe he bleeding downstairs on my basement floor," Mario said, standing behind him with the gun at the back of his head.

"What you gon' do, Mario? Kill me because I let your bitch suck me off?"

"For that and for you and your bitch ass friend trynna rob my family. But I wanna see your face before I blow your ass all the way back to west bumafuck." He pulled the mask off and I was shocked.

"That's him, Mario. That's the guy that raped me with his friends."

"Oh yeah? Well, isn't this a coincidence. How do you suppose we handle this, baby girl?"

"I got this." I cocked my pistol and shot him right in the middle of his forehead. I stood over him and Mario stood next to me. I emptied my clip and Mario shot off two rounds.

"Dad, it's time to go," he said. His father got up and rolled up his sleeves. "Call Rocko and tell him to get the van. Desi, you and the other ladies clean up this mess. We about to take a ride."

"I know, Babe. I got this." I helped Mario and his dad wrap the bodies up and as soon as Rocko pulled into the garage, we loaded the bodies and they drove off. The other women and I cleaned up the mess like this was a part of our daily lives. Well, it was for me because this wasn't the first time. The first time this happened, it was this dude named Duke whose blood I had to clean. He had to be taught a lesson and shown as an example for people that wanted to try to steal product from Mario and his boys.

Once Mario got back, it was time for everyone to leave. I was tired so it was time to start kicking people out. I wanted to clean up our house, shower and go to bed. By the time everything was said and done, it was going on three in the morning. As soon as I got out the shower, I got into the bed.

"Baby, are you okay?" Mario asked as he rubbed on my head as I laid on his chest.

"Yeah, I'm good, Boo. Why you ask that?"

"You just seem kind of distant since we had to handle business."

"Naw, I'm good, Babe. I just been thinking about how much I loved you and how I never wanted to be without you. I love the way we protect each other and work as a team."

"You're so sweet. I love you too. Good night, Boo."

"Good night, Mario." He kissed me on the forehead and held me as we both fell into a deep slumber that was much needed after a night like this.

****

Nymphopervtress

I was glad to see the rays from the morning sun shine through the window. I had been tossing and turning all night long because of what happened last night. I looked at the time and it was one in the afternoon. I turned towards Mario. He was gone. I got up and slipped on one of his shirts before heading downstairs. Wasn't there. I checked the garage and the basement and there were still no signs of him. Where the hell was he? I didn't come across a note or anything. He always left a note for me. I called his cell phone and it went straight to voicemail. I was starting to get worried. I called his parents and they didn't hear anything from him since last night. His mom told me to give her a call if I hear from him and I told her okay.

I called Jay and he kept sending me to voicemail. I quickly showered and dressed. I hopped in my car and went on a search for my man. I searched all of his drug spots looking for him—the liquor store, even some of the stores that I knew he frequented daily. As I rode through some abandoned-looking streets, on the verge of giving up, I spotted his truck. I read the license plate to confirm and I was right. I parked my car behind his and jumped out. I knocked on the door that looked like it had a little life left in it. The door swung open and one of his boys named Tim Tim stood before me.

"Hey, Tim Tim, where is Mario?"

"Downstairs, handling something."

"Handling what? I been trying to contact him all morning."

"Some dude tried to stick him up. So, he's down there teaching him a lesson."

"I'm going down there." I pushed past him. He wasn't just gonna get rid of me like that. I would make up a lie to tell Mario so he could fuck him up if it had come to it. I looked in the living room and den areas before checking the kitchen. He wasn't there so I headed downstairs.

"I hope you learned to stop trying to stick up people after this," I heard Mario say. His statement was followed by hefty laughs from his goons. I followed the voices. They were coming from the end of the hall. I walked steadfastly to the bedroom and swung open the door. It was pure shock on my face when I saw what was going on before my eyes.

Mario had some guy handcuffed to the leg of a table. They were all taking turns fucking him in the ass and making him suck their dicks. Mario was up in his ass just like he be in mine. I gasped. All eyes were on me.

"Boo, it's not what you think," he said while he still had his dick in the guy's asshole. I looked to the guy that had a dick stuck in his mouth and started to cry. I cried for him. I cried for me.

"What am I thinking, Mario? What should I be thinking?"

"It's not what you think," he repeated.

"So I don't see my man sticking his dick in some nigga's ass is what you're telling me, right? This is a mirage I'm having, right?"

"No, you're not having a mirage, Boo," he said, finally getting up from his knees and pulling up his pants.

"Don't touch me," I yelled when he tried to touch me.

"Baby, please. I'm just working."

"Yeah, I can see that. That's how you work with me too."

"This is just business. This guy tried to rob me. Thought your man was sweet for it."

"I don't give a damn what he did. Why are you fucking him and making it seem like you were enjoying it? You're gay and there is no way around it."

"I'm not gay, Boo. I love women. I love you. Please just understand. We just teaching him a lesson about trying to stick people up."

"So y'all decided to stick dicks up his ass?"

"So you understand the concept?"

"I'm out of here," I said. I took my engagement ring off and threw it at his chest. I ran up the basement steps in tears.

"Desi! Desiree," I heard him yell after me. I never looked back. Tim Tim let me out the door and I ran to my car. By the time I started the car, I saw Mario run out the house, heading towards me. I put the car in drive and sped off.

I looked in the rearview and saw him standing on the sidewalk where I left him. He adjusted his dick in his pants and headed back in the house.

Chapter Twenty-Two:
Unbreak My Heart

It had been days since I had seen Mario fucking another man. I had gone to our house and took all of my clothes and belongings out in record time. I came straight to my mother's house. My safe haven. Mario had sent endless text messages and a slew of calls. I sent every one of them to voicemail.

I didn't know what he was going to say. I didn't know what to say to him. I don't even know why he continued to blow up my phone. There was no way in hell he was going to be able to explain this. I wasn't supposed to be upset with him. He was my boo and he did this shit to me. I am teaching him a lesson. I recited in my head. He could have easily told me that he was gay or bi-sexual or whatever he was. This shit was crazy. I heard a knock at the door. I didn't answer it or anything but they still opened the door. My little sister peeked her head in.

"Can I come in, Desi?"

"Yeah," I said. No matter what was going on in my life I always felt a lot better when my sister was around.

"Are you okay, sis?"

"I will be," I said, wiping my eyes.

"That's good. I'm sorry about you and Mario, Desi. But it will get better."

"I know."

"I'm always gonna be here for you to talk to me. You know that, right?"

"Yes, I do," I said, hugging her.

"Okay, now that we done had our mushy moment, I need to find something to do today," she said, hopping up off the bed and heading towards the door.

"I know what we can do."

"What?"

"Go have a girl's day out."

"That sounds fun. Let me go get my purse and I will be ready in ten."

"Well, I have to shower and beautify myself before I hit the streets."

"Good luck with that. You look like a Raggedy Ann doll," she said, laughing. I threw a pillow at her and laughed. It felt good to laugh for a change.

This was always the medicine that helped me get through whatever I had going on in my life. I got in the shower and it felt so damn good. The steaming hot waterfall was raining down on my body and numbing my pain. I turned off the cold water so the water would be scorching hot. I just stood under the shower head and let the water burn all the way down to my soul. I eventually cleaned my body and got out after three washes. I moisturized my body as I usually did and got dressed. I decided on some skinny jeans, a light sweater, and some Ugg boots to match. I grabbed my leather jacket and grabbed my keys.

"Come on, slow poke," I said, banging on Monet's door.

"I'm coming, I'm coming," my sister said, from the other side of the door. Her door swung open and luckily she was still dressed. As long as I took, I thought she was gonna put her chill out clothes on. We went out the door and headed to mall. I couldn't wait until we got to the mall. I had to do some much needed stress shopping.

We were having so much fun and my spirit was trying to lift. We had only been here for about two hours and I was feeling glad that I escaped the house for a little while. We managed to pick up a couple of things for our mom and each other and now we were in the jewelry store. We walked in and I picked out a beautiful necklace for my mom. I let my sister pick out the one she wanted and I bought it. I was scanning over the expensive pieces to see what I wanted to purchase for myself when I bumped into somebody.

"Oh, excuse me," I said politely.

"You better excuse yourself," the lady said. I looked into her face and it was Lexi.

"Oh, it's you? I don't know why you're here with your broke ass. Rainbow is right across the hall."

"Oh cute, real cute. I'm just in here shopping for Mario's Christmas present," she said, smiling.

"Good for you. So am I," I lied. "But you know with your little welfare check, $300 can't go but so far. I'm just saying," I said, folding my arms.

"Oh, you got jokes I see. I got one for you. What's bruised, bloody, and unconscious?" she asked with a devilish grin on her face.

"I don't know," I responded. My sister had heard the commotion and came over beside me.

"Oh goodie, we have an audience to hear the joke too. Well, the answer to the joke is you, Destiny."

"Bitch. My name is Desiree and I don't see how that joke refers to me."

"Well, let me break it down for you. When you got raped you got both beat the fuck up and you damn near bled to death when you had a miscarriage.

Nymphopervtress

Need I say more?"

I looked at her in astonishment. "How do you know all of this?" I asked, through clenched teeth.

"Duh, I was there. I set up the whole thing. I know you didn't tell Mario the truth but I can't wait to tell him. I got everything on video."

I couldn't believe what I was hearing. This stupid hating-ass-hoe was the reason this shit happened? Oh fuck no. I reached up and slapped the hell out of her. She fell over and I grabbed her by her nappy ass tracks. I slammed her face onto the glass counter so damn hard it cracked.

"Hey, hey. No fighting in the store. Get out," the salesman yelled. I wrapped her hair around my hand and dragged her out the store with my sister in tow. I punched and kicked her and threw her up against store windows and railings. I noticed an audience of people gathering but I didn't care. I was whooping her ass for all the pain she caused. She was the reason I got raped. And she was the reason I lost my child. This bitch had to die.

"Go get the car!" I yelled at my sister and threw the keys at her. She caught them and ran out the mall. I eventually got tired of whooping this bitch's ass so I just let her drop to the floor. She was no match for me. I kicked her a couple more times in her face and stomach before spitting on her and leaving. Someone was bound to call the cops and I didn't need that heat right now. When I got outside, my savior was right there with the car running. I jumped in and we sped off. "Take me to Mario's house."

****

"Hey, Baby," Mario said when he saw me at the door. He opened his arms wide and I pushed them out the way as I went into the house.

"Don't you 'hey baby' me. I saw your little bitch today. So I guess y'all back fucking around since she's buying gifts and shit. Am I right?"

"What are you talking about, Desi? I'm not talking to anybody, Boo. I've been too busy working and trying to get you to come back home."

"I'm talking about that hoe, Lexi. I seen her while I was at the mall and shit and she started talking out the side of her face. So I fucked her up."

"I'm so sorry you had to do that," he said, shaking his head. I started to cry a little bit. "What's wrong, Boo?" he asked.

I sniffled. "That bitch set me up."

"What you mean set you up? How did she set you up?"

"She was the reason I got raped and why I miscarried and lost the baby." I saw pure anger and hatred wash over his face. He grabbed me and held me. I broke all the way down. I missed this. I missed my baby. Just in this instant, it made me want him back. I needed him back in my life indefinitely.

"I'm gonna take care of that bitch, Boo. I told you no matter what I was gonna always be here for you and protect you."

"I want you back, Mario," I whispered into his chest.

"I never went nowhere, baby girl. I'm here. I'm gonna always be right here. I'm sorry for what I did to you, Desiree. Look at me." I looked up into his eyes. "I am not gay, okay? I was just teaching that guy a lesson. Do you believe me?"

I shook my head yes. For the life of me, I hope he was being honest. It would hurt even more if I found out he was lying. But after all I have done behind closed doors, he probably would have put me on the chopping block. I would've been walking around with an 'X' on my back, waiting to get murked.

Mario and I had reconciled and now we were just chilling. We ate and we watched a couple of movies. Just like the good ol' times. I really missed this part of our relationship. "You ready to go home?" he asked me as he rubbed my shoulder.

I looked at him right in his eyes. "I'm already home."

"Welcome back."

"I'm glad to be back." I laid back on the sofa and he got on top of me. He lay on top of me and kissed me ever so gently. He removed both of our clothes from our bodies then took me to the kitchen. He sat me on top of the kitchen table and sat a chair right in front of me. He sat down and threw my legs over his shoulders so he could feast. My sweet nectar started to drip from me and I started moaning as I grabbed his hair. I pushed his face deeper between my thighs before coming all over his face. I had come so hard, I heard it dripping on the floor. He picked me up and took me upstairs. There, in our private lair, he made sweet passionate love to me like he would never see me again.

****

I woke up and looked around. It felt good to be back here for the most part. I looked over and Mario wasn't there. I saw a note on the bed:
'I love you, Desiree, and I will always and forever protect you. The job is done so you have no more to worry about or have to stress over Lexi. Come downstairs after you read this. Make sure you wash your face and brush your teeth. LOL Love Always and Forever, Mario'

He was such a cornball but he was my cornball and I loved him with all my heart. I went to go do my morning ritual then headed downstairs. I walked into a room full of rose bouquets flooding the entire living room. I saw Mario at the bottom of the stairs dressed like a waiter. I just smiled and giggled.

"What is going on, Mario?" I asked giving him his usual morning kiss.

"Good morning, Mrs. Davis," he responded playing the role. "I have a breakfast spread laid out for you this morning."

"Oh yeah? Then why are we standing here? I'm hungry," I responded, pulling his arm. We made our way to the kitchen and the table looked beautiful. All the food was spread out like a buffet and I couldn't wait. "Aren't you gonna join me, Boo?"

"Hell yeah. I ain't cook all of this for you. I made you some cereal." He said, laughing. I missed that laugh. He sat down and we ate. We feasted on steak, eggs, hash browns, waffles, bacon, apple sauce, sausage and orange juice. The breakfast was great. Mario stood over top of me with a silver tray covered up.

"No more food, Mario, please. I'm stuffed."

"I am too, but please." He placed the tray down and I uncovered it. A small velvet box was sitting in the middle. I opened it and there was my engagement ring along with another ring underneath. I slipped my engagement ring back on. And I picked up the other ring. It was engraved on the inside and the outside. The inside read: Desiree and Mario. It had two hearts by each name. The outside said: Forever Yours. I teared up and looked at him.

"I love you, Mario."

"I love you too, Desiree." I stood up and kissed him deeply. We headed upstairs back to our room. We had a quick session before falling back to sleep from eating all that damn food. I was finally back home and my heart felt full again.

Chapter Twenty-Three:
Ride Or Die

"I need you, Boo," Mario said to me a few days later. We were sitting in the truck outside of the house.

"I need you too," I said rubbing on his thigh. He smiled and licked his lips.

"As tempting as that is right now, baby girl, I need you on my team. I need to take down some men."

"So what do you need me for?"

"Bait."

"Bait? What kind of bait?"

"You're beautiful, you're smart, and you can catch any man's eye."

"Okay."

"I need you to put on your charm along with your tightest outfit and help me take down these niggas that's been trying to move into our territory."

"That sounds a little dangerous, Mario."

"Ride or die?"

"I'm gon' ride."

"Then ride with me. Go change your clothes and come back. The fellas are waiting on us now."

I got out the car and ran into the house. I decided on wearing a skin-tight knit dress. It was just right for this weather. I put on my five inch black heels and went to the bathroom. I touched up my hair and makeup before leaving out. I headed back to the truck and hopped back in. Mario was ending a call.

"You looking good, Boo."

"Thanks."

"This is gonna be easier than I thought," he said, laughing as he pulled off. We drove for about thirty minutes and parked after circling the block a couple of times.

Once we parked, I noticed Rocko, Tim Tim, and Slim parked across the street from us.

"Now listen, baby girl, the house you're going to is three doors down from here."

"So why are we parked right here, Babe?"

"So those niggas won't see us coming. I want you to walk over and knock on the door. Ask them if you can use their phone to call AAA because your keys got locked in the car and so did your cell."

"Okay. But what if he doesn't believe me?"

"Oh he will. And then we gonna come around the back way and bust up in there. So when you hear us, I want you to pretend like you don't know what's going on. Act surprised and scared."

"Okay. Got it, Mario." He kissed me and I got out. I walked up a few steps and I looked back. Mario and his boys were getting out of their vehicles and heading around back. I reached the doorstep and took a deep breath before knocking. A skinny little dude answered.

"Hey, I'm sorry to bother you but may I use your phone to call AAA please?"

"What's wrong, lil mama?" he said in a southern accent.

"Me, moving too fast, I locked my keys and stuff in the car and I had to walk two blocks because nobody would let me use theirs or they weren't home," I said, lying. I was playing the part extremely well.

"Sure, come on in." He stepped aside and let me through. He pointed me to the direction of the phone that was on the table. I sat down and pretended to dial a number. "You sure are pretty," he said, sitting down next to me.

"Thank you," I responded moving over a little. And he moved closer.

"You know you can wait here while AAA comes."

"No, thanks. I'm good," I said, standing up. "Hello, this is Amber Holly and I was calling because I need help getting my keys out," I said, when the operator came on. He came up behind me and rubbed up against me. "Can you stop please?"

"Yeah, I can. But who's to say I will?"

Bang.

We both turned our head to where there was once a door but now it was on the floor. Mario and his boys were masked and had guns drawn. "Put y'all motherfucking hands up," Slim yelled at me and the guy.

"What the fuck is this?" the guy asked.

"This is a hit, you bitch ass nigga. I told you don't fuck with me and my team, son." Mario hit him in the head with the gun. As hard as the impact was, it caused the dude to fall right to the floor. I could see where he had been hit because it was already starting to swell.

Rocko came over to me and grabbed me around my neck from behind. "Is this your bitch?" he asked the dude with the gun up to my head. I could feel him pushing his body into mine. That wasn't part of the plan. I said aloud in my head.

"No, I'm not," I said, trying to act like he was really hurting me.

"Naw, she ain't. She ain't got nothing to do with this."

"Well, now she does. She here, ain't she?"

"We gonna take the bitch with us," Mario said to Rocko. "We can have some fun with her." He looked at Slim. "Case the place, Dawg." Slim hurriedly did as his Boss had said. "Now you, next time don't fuck with me. My bad, it ain't gonna be a next time." He pointed the gun between the man's eyes and shot him. His head split open like a damn banana.

Slim came back down with a duffel bag. Mario scooped me up and we all ran out the back door. When we got around to the street, we all started acting casual like we didn't just kill a man. We jumped in our cars and headed to me and Mario's house.

"Are you okay?" Mario asked, because I had spaced out.

"Yeah, I'm good, Baby. No worries."

"Good. So I'm gonna need you again for more jobs like that."

"I'm here for you, Boo."

"That's my girl," he said, rubbing my knee.

Truth be told, the killing gave me some type of rush. It turned me on to be in charge of somebody's fate. I started shifting in my seat. Mario looked over at me.

"What's wrong, Desi?"

"Nothing. I need a hand."

"With what?"

"No. I meant I need your hand. Right now," I said. He gave me his hand and I opened my legs up and put his hand between them. "Play with me, Daddy." He stuck his fingers inside me and fingered me until I lightly came on his fingers. I sucked the juices from each one before setting it back on his lap.

"You know, I'm getting in that pussy as soon as we get home."

"You gotta take care of business first."

"That is part of my business."

We got home ten minutes later. While Rocko and Slim sat downstairs watching the NBA highlights, Mario and I went upstairs for a quickie. And a quickie it was. We came back down the stairs fifteen minutes later. He and the guys went to the basement to discuss business and I took a nap. Today was a long and stressful day. But overall, I enjoyed being a part of one of Mario's hits.

****

Nymphopervtress

It's going on the third week for me being the bait for Mario. It's been hectic but very rewarding. Since I had been working and doing jobs, I received a new mink, a new diamond necklace, a new Dodge Charger, and even got paid. My bank account held a whopping $10,000. That's from the previous jobs as well as me saving some of the money he had been giving me over time. Today's job was gonna be extra crazy. This time they wanted to rob a dominant. He wanted me to pretend that I was interested in being his slave. I didn't know about that.

"Why do I have to do it, Mario?"

"Because he got that bag. Do you realize how much money somebody like him makes daily satisfying the crazy fantasies of women?"

"No, I don't, but what am I supposed to do?"

"Well, participate of course," he said frankly.

"What do I wear?"

"I already got that taken care of so don't worry about that. I got you the perfect costume picked out upstairs."

"Okay." I couldn't even go against what he asked. It's not like I was doing this for free. For all I knew, I would enjoy it. You never know. I have never been a slave but I have seen it on S&M porn. I found it intriguing. And on top of that, reading about it was a turn on as well. I looked at the clock. It was 9:00. It was time to get ready for my session that was scheduled for 10.

After I got dressed, I looked over myself in the mirror. A leather strappy fishnet body suit and five inch studded heels adorned my body. I looked good and I felt good. So why was my stomach doing flips? I had to wash away that nervousness before going into the guy's place. Mario came in the room and checked me out.

"We should do some dominatrix shit if you gonna be looking that good. You can tie me up anytime."

"I might just take you up on that offer, Mario," I said grabbing my new wig off the bed. I fixed it and observed again. I looked like a totally different person which was good. I didn't want anyone to recognize me if I had been seen. We went down the stairs and headed to the car. This time we rode in the car with Slim and Rocko. We went over the plan one last time to make sure everybody knew their job. Once we all agreed, we parked and I got ready to get out.

"Be careful, baby girl," Mario said kissing me on the cheek.

"Always," I responded and stepped out. I headed down the block to the seedy-looking house and knocked on the door.

"Who the hell is it?" said an angry voice from the other side of the door.

"It's Kate," I said, giving him one of my alias'. I heard five locks unlock before the door opened.

"Hey, you're on time," he said, opening the door and letting me in. "I see you already came prepared. You look great and I can't wait to tie you up." He led me down to the basement and I instantly got scared. It looked like I had walked right into a midcentury dungeon. There were shackles for hands and feet on one wall. A table that held different sizes of belts, paddles, whips, chains, and stuff for gagging people. In the middle of the room, there was a chair. It looked like a dentist chair minus the stirrups that was attached to the end of it. "What were you doing getting sent to my office today?"

"What?" I asked.

"I said what were you doing getting sent to my office today. Don't make me ask you a third time, young lady."

I forgot what was going on for a second. Then I quickly switched to role playing mode. "I was being bad in class," I replied.

"I know that. And then your teacher tells me you were in there showing your breasts to some guy in the back of the class. Why did you do that?" he asked as he picked up a paddle from the table. He walked over to me and was slapping his hand with it. He was impatiently waiting for an answer.

"He asked to see them, sir. It was only for a couple of minutes."

"So what does that mean? I want you to show me your breasts. Right now," he said. I pulled the front of my body suit down and exposed my big breasts. He grabbed one and massaged it. "Get over there and bend over that chair. You need to be taught a lesson." I walked over to the chair and bent over like he ordered. He hit me once with the paddle. Then another. By the time he hit my ass the fifth time with the paddle, my pain had subsided and turned into pleasure. Now I was able to enjoy myself. But then I thought, where the hell was Mario?

The weird dominant then put me in shackles and hit me with the whip a couple of times. The pain felt so good that I had come and it was running down my legs. He fell to his knees and licked the cum off my thighs. He put his face in my crotch and cleaned up the excess cum with his mouth. We heard a door come crashing down the stairs. Mario was here.

They all came running down the stairs. Rocko grabbed him and Slim searched the place. Mario walked over in a slow motion movement, tapping his gun on his side as he came. "Well, well, well. What do we have here?"

"Mario, what the fuck do you want?"

"Remember I told you I was gonna meet up with you again one day, Ricardo. I want the money."

"I don't have any." Mario slapped him with the gun and snatched him up by the collar on his neck.

"Don't fucking play with me, Ricardo. I know you. Now you're either gonna tell my boys where you keep your money or I'm gonna pop a hot one in you and find it myself. Which would you prefer?"

"It's under the floor boards," he said, pointing to the floor.

"Rock get that shit. Ricardo hand me the key so I can let my girl out."

"Your girl? You set me up, motherfucker?"

"Not necessarily. I knew with your horny and fetish ways you couldn't resist." He released me and I walked back over to Ricardo with him. I had drawn my gun that I had inside my purse. Rocko came back with a trash bag full of money. "We good?"

"Yeah, we good," Rocko replied.

"Get down on your knees," Mario said, as he pushed the gun into Ricardo's temple. I had my gun still drawn on him as well.

"I thought you were gonna let me live. You lied, Mario," he cried. He begged and pleaded for his life.

"I am gonna let you live."

"Thank you," he said.

"But I'm not," I said, pulling the trigger on my gun. His body flew back on the floor and went still. Slim and Rocko rolled the body up and put it inside a trash can. They carried it out the back door that they had come through. We walked to the street and I noticed a truck that I didn't notice the first time we got here. The guys put the can in the back of the truck and Mario and I got back in the car we had come in.

"So are you good, Boo?"

"Yeah, I'm straight, Mario. Just wanna get home and take a shower. I'm really tired."

"Okay, no problem."

We drove home in silence. Mainly because I had dozed off to sleep. When I woke up, we were pulling into the driveway. "We're home, sleepy head," Mario said. We got out the car and I headed straight for the shower. I let the shower water run while I got a tank top and some boy shorts to sleep in. I grabbed my things and took them in the bathroom. I was looking in the mirror when I felt something coming up my throat. I quickly leaned over the toilet and emptied the contents of my stomach into the commode. I wiped my mouth and brushed my teeth before getting in the shower. I cleansed my body and washed my sins from my head down to my feet. I towel-dried my body and got my clothes on. I went and jumped in the bed, next to Mario.

"You good, Desiree?"

"Yeah, I'm good, baby. I love you," I said, giving him a little peck on the lips.

"I love you too."

Chapter Twenty-Four:
Laugh Now, Cry Later

❧

As soon as I got to Shannon's house, I ran to the bathroom and took out the pregnancy test.

"Girl, slow down," she yelled from behind me.

"I can't Shannon. I gotta know if I'm pregnant again."

"Just don't stress yourself no matter what the test says."

"Okay." I went into the bathroom and peed on the stick. Time to wait. I left the bathroom and sat next to Shannon on the bed. "Well, what do you wanna do while we wait?"

"Well, we can take your mind off of things."

"That's the same thing I was thinking," I said, smiling at her. I ran my fingers through her hair and pulled her close to me. Our lips met and parted. I kissed her and she put her hands under my shirt. She played with my nipples making them hard. It had become like a second nature for me to sneak around with Shannon some days, and Jessica, the other days. It's not like Mario would get mad if I was sneaking around with a woman anyway. He would probably more than likely join in like before.

She took my shirt off and removed my bra. She buried her face between my breasts and I moaned. "Oh shit. Shannon that feels good. Suck on my nipples, Baby."

"I wanna suck on that pussy," she said, removing my jeans. She pulled my panties to the side and licked the inside of my pussy. She and I were enjoying it so much and eventually I came. She didn't even wanna do anything else. So I just left my pants on the floor and went to check my test.

I walked to the bathroom and picked it up off the sink. It read 'pregnant.' I was a happy about that. At first, I thought I had a stomach virus or something. I showed Shannon the test and she smiled. "Well, you're gonna have a baby now after all," she said. She led me back to the bed and had me lie down. She put on her strap on dick and got on top of me. She inserted her penis inside me and stuck it in deeply. We both moaned together and kissed each other throughout the entire ordeal. We rolled over and I ended up on top. I rode that toy like it was the real thing. I hopped up and down on it, rotated on it, and even did a reverse cowgirl position on it. I played with my clit as I fucked Shannon and I squirted all over her. She lifted me up, off her dick and placed me over her face where she caught the rest of my cum. We laid in the bed next to each other and fell asleep.

I had awoken to the sound of my phone ringing. It was Mario calling me. "What's up, Boo?" I said.

"That's what I would like to know."

"What are you talking about now, Mario?"

"Where are you? I have been calling you for hours."

"I'm over Shannon's house. I been here all day."

"Doing what? What could you have possibly been doing all day that you couldn't answer my calls or anything?"

"Just chilling, Bae, that's all."

"Yeah, I bet. You probably over there fucking. Ain't you?"

"No, Mario. I'm laying down. I just woke up."

"Mmhmm I hear you. What time will you be home?"

"On my way now."

"Don't bother. Just chill with your girl."

"What's wrong, Mario?"

"Nothing. Imma see you when you get home." He hung up.

I didn't understand what the hell that was about but I wasn't gonna trip off of it either. I put my pants on and went to look for Shannon. She was in the basement playing her Xbox One. "Something is wrong, Shannon," I said when I saw her.

"Something like what?"

"Mario called and was acting a little weird. I told him I was about to come home and he told me no."

"That's because he probably not home."

"Then where would he be?"

"Out running the streets."

"Oh no. I don't believe that Shannon," I said with a laugh.

"You sure about that?"

"Yes," I said. Deep down I was hoping and praying she was wrong.

"Okay let's go," she said turning off her game.

"Where are we going?"

"To find your man, duh. That nigga is not home and I'm gonna prove it to you."

"Be my guest," I said with confidence. I knew Mario. He wouldn't be out doing something wrong. That's what I did. But I wasn't worried about that right now. I pulled out my phone and tracked his. He was at home. "He at the house, Shannon."

"Okay, come on. We can take my uncle's car. He won't mind." We hopped in the little Toyota Camry and drove to my house. I could see the upstairs light on in the bedroom. "How are we gonna get up there without him knowing you're home?"

"We can go through the basement. I got the key hidden under a rock."

"Cool." We tiptoed around to the back of the house, making sure not to step on any leaves or twigs. I unlocked the basement door and gently opened and closed the door. We took our shoes off and headed up the stairs. I could hear him moaning. He was probably watching a porn. It was part of his nightly ritual. But then I heard a female voice say "Do you like that, Daddy?" That threw me off for a second. I kicked the door open and stood there in pure shock and disbelief.

Mario had a bitch under the blanket sucking his dick! I snatched the blanket off the bed and discovered it was Lexi. "Desiree? Baby, calm down, please." I ain't hear shit he was saying out his mouth.

My eyes started to water as I looked back and forth between the two. "Come on, Desi," Shannon said trying to pull me out the room by my arm. I just stood there like dead weight. Like a flash of lightening, I flipped out and jumped on the bed. Mario moved out the way and I pounced on Lexi's ass. I pounded and pounded her face trying to break her fucking nose. I was so damn heated. I threw her on the floor and I kicked her in the head. She tried to crawl away but Shannon dragged her right back over to me. I looked over to Mario. My heart had shattered into a million pieces in an instant.

"Desiree, baby, I'm sorry."

"Yeah, you are sorry. But I'm not, Mario." I threw both rings at him that he had given me. I went to the closet and packed some clothes.

"Where are you going, Desiree?" he asked, pulling on my suitcase.

"Doesn't matter. I'm leaving here, that's for damn sure. Shannon, can you help me please?"

"Yeah, sure." She took my bags and headed downstairs. "It's nice to know that you were still fucking around with her. Makes me know that I wouldn't even be able to trust you with our baby."

"What? What are you talking about?"

"Our baby, motherfucker," I said, throwing the pregnancy test at him. He looked at it then looked at me. I turned and walked out. He called my name and I just kept going. I got into Shannon's car and we rolled out.

She took me to a hotel and she stayed there with me. Just think that just this morning, I was full of laughs and happiness. And now I was full of tears and pain. I guess that's the way love goes.

Chapter Twenty-Five:
Before The Sunrise

I have been locked up in this hotel for two weeks. No visitors. No calls. Not even a proper shower. It feels like my whole life is worthless now that Mario is not a part of it anymore. I have been having a self-pity party and forgetting somebody very important: my unborn child. He or she needed me. They needed me to be strong so I can get through this with or without Mario in my life. I needed to wake my ass the fuck up and snap back to reality. I laid on the bed for a few more minutes before finally getting up. I went to use the bathroom and relieve myself of my morning sickness. Once it was all out of my system, I called the doctor. They gave me an appointment for Friday at ten. I checked my voicemails and my text messages. Seventy-five in total.

My mom and sister blew me up as well as my girls. But nobody blew me up more than Mario had. I read all of his texts and they all said mainly the same thing: 'I'm sorry, Desi' 'forgive me baby' 'I love you'. Blah blah blah. I was tired of his bullshit. I just wanted him there for the baby, just that. After the incident that took place, I shouldn't even allow him to have any parts of this pregnancy. I don't give a damn if he's the father or not. He betrayed me and he humiliated me. In the back of my head, my conscience was telling me that I was doing the same thing. In actuality, I wasn't. I didn't get caught and I don't plan on it either.

I texted Mario and he texted back:

Me: I have a doc appt @ 10 Friday
Mario: need me to take you?
Me: no. just be at PG by 10
Mario: I wanna c u
Me: u will c me Friday
Mario: I wanna c u now. Wya?
Me: in my skin. Bye Mario
Mario: I love you, Desiree
Me: sure you do. Ttyl

I was tired of his bullshit. You know what else I was tired of right now? Being lonely. Mario was making sure he got his rocks off so why couldn't I worry about mine? I didn't feel like searching for anybody but I did anyway. I inboxed some guy named Leon and told him to meet me at the hotel I was at. He said okay and I told him to text me his room number and I will be there. Thirty minutes later, I received a text from him saying he was in room 304. That was only two floors down. Of course he didn't know that. I washed up really good and put on a bra and panty set with a trench coat. I left my room and slipped onto the elevator.

I got to his floor and searched for room 304. Once I located it, I knocked on the door. A tall caramel guy who looked to be about 6'6 opened the door for me. "You must be Jazmin," he said.

"Yes. Nice to meet you, Leon. Can I come in?"

"Sure. Make yourself at home if you want."

"I think I will," I said, taking off my trench coat. It dropped to the floor and so did his mouth. I did a sexy walk to where he was. I pushed him against the door and ripped his shirt open. I sucked on his right nipple and flicked the left. "Play with my pussy," I said into his ear. He quickly stuck his hand inside my panties and put two fingers in my pussy. I put my foot up on a chair so he could push his fingers in a little deeper. I came on his fingers and then I moved his hand. I squatted down in front of him and undid his jeans. I let them drop to the floor and he stepped out of them. He leaned back up against the door and I took him into my mouth.

It's been a while since I had a dick in my mouth and it felt a little awkward. But as soon as I got into the rhythm of it, I was back on my game. I placed each one of his hands on either side of my head and had him fuck my face. I could feel half of his dick going down my throat. I felt like the sword swallower. Once he got rock hard, I took him over to the bed. He took a condom out of his pants pocket off the floor and put it on. I jumped right on top without hesitation. I rode that dick as if it were my own. Like my name was branded on this meat. He flipped the position and laid me on my back.

He put each one of my legs in his hand and spread them in the air. He fucked me gently with deep strokes. He was giving me them 'I want you to have my baby' strokes. I came all over him and he busted his nut inside the condom. When he went to the bathroom to clean up and pee, I grabbed my trench coat and slipped out the door unnoticed. I took off my shoes so I could run up the stairwell to my room. I didn't wanna take the elevator and chance him seeing me and finding out I lived there. Not that it was any of his business, but I had to make sure.

I had gotten back to my room and showered all over again. I decided to go see my mom. That's the least I could do since I missed all the holidays with her. I just needed to sit down and talk with her. I missed her. My sister was away for the week so I couldn't see her but I would call her later and check up on her.

I had checked the weather and it was not a normal mid-January temperature. It was gonna be seventy degrees today. Mother Nature really needed to make up her mind about this weather. I decided to wear some jeans and my Timbs today. I threw on a t-shirt and a jean jacket. I looked in the mirror and my hair looked jacked. I brushed and combed it out before dropping like a pound of moisturizer and jam in it. I brushed it back into a ponytail and I was good. It was great to be natural sometimes. I grabbed my wallet, my phone, and my room key and headed to the garage.

I felt an eerie feeling wash over me as soon as I went out the hotel door to the garage. It felt like I was being watched. Like I was being followed. I kept looking back but nobody was there. Just my footsteps. When I reached my car, I realized that those weren't just my footsteps that entire time. I jumped in my car and immediately locked the doors. I started the car and sat a few moments to find a radio station. This was force of habit no doubt. Once I found some music playing, I reached over and grabbed my seat belt. I jumped out of my skin when I saw somebody just standing there looking in my window.

"Open the door, Desiree." It was Mario. He looked horrible. It looked as if he hadn't shaved or showered in weeks. And his bloodshot eyes didn't help the situation. I didn't move a muscle. I looked at him and he looked back at me. I was trying to read him but I couldn't. All I could see in his eyes were hatred and pain. That was exactly how I felt within my heart. "I said open the door, Desiree," he said again. I was about to reach for the button to pop the lock open, when I noticed his gun in his hand. I panicked so I just quickly put the car in reverse and backed out. I sped off and headed out the parking lot. Two gun shots rang out as I turned the corner. This nigga was trying to kill me. How did he even know where to find me?

I drove like a bat out of hell, trying to get to my mother's house. I pulled up to my mother's house fifteen minutes later. I was surprised I didn't get a ticket as fast as I was driving. I was getting ready to get out of my car when I noticed an out-of-place van pulling up behind me. I squinted my eyes in my rearview mirror to see if I could see anything. Nothing. I didn't want to bring nothing bad to my mother's house so I put my seat belt back on and turned my engine back on. I drove away and so did they.

I quickly called my mother. "Ma, somebody is following me."

"Following you? What did you do?"

"Nothing. This creepy van parked behind me when I was outside your house and now they following me."

"Well, call the police."

I hung up the phone and quickly dialed 911.

"What is the location of the emergency?" the operator said.

"I'm on Marlboro Pike."

"What's the problem?"

"Somebody is following me. Tell the cops to meet me at the Redskins Stadium gate 132B. I'm heading that way now!"

"I will dispatch some officers, ma'am. What is your name?"

"Desiree Logan."

"Okay, I got it and I will put this through."

I hung up on her and headed towards the Redskins Stadium. I looked in the rearview and the van was still there. I didn't know what the hell to think. This shit was absurd. I didn't know what the hell was going on. By the time I got to gate 132B, there was still no sign of the cops. I just stopped driving. I had given up. The truck parked a few feet away from me. As soon as I was getting ready to exit the vehicle and confront this stalker, a slew of police cars came flying from every direction. The truck attempted to move but he was unsuccessful. They had him surrounded. There was nowhere to run.

"Step out of the vehicle," one officer yelled through a bullhorn. Another officer came over to me and asked me if I was ok and I said yes.

The driver side door swung open and I saw two feet hit the ground. Shots were fired as the driver came around the door. He shot and the police shot. I ducked down behind my car so I wouldn't get hit by any stray bullets. He must have been wearing a bullet proof vest because he was getting hit but there was no impact. I guess only one cop was smart enough to notice that because she shot him in the leg and he went down.

The fire ceased. Everyone went over to see who it was and so did I. They stood him up and took off his mask. "Do you know who this is, ma'am?"

I was appalled. It was Scott. "Yes, sir. His name is Scott Manor." I hung my head down.

"Let's go, asshole." The police officer handcuffed him and threw him in the back of a car. I guess he was like damn the paramedics.

"We're gonna need for you to come down to the station to answer some questions, ma'am."

"Okay," I responded. I got in my car and headed to Barlowe Road.

****

They were driving me crazy at this damn precinct. Asking me a million and one damn questions that I barely knew answers to. They finally sent a detective in to ask more questions. What a day.

"Hello, Ms. Logan. My name is Detective Herrod. I will be asking a few questions. I will be manually recording our conversation versus using a tape recorder. If it seems like I'm not paying attention just know I am. I'm just gonna write down everything you say to the following questions. Do you understand?"

"Yes, sir."

"Okay good. Now for the record, can you state your whole name for me?"

"Desiree Michelle Logan."

"How old are you?"

"18."

"Where do you work?"

"I'm in between jobs right now."

He stopped talking and was writing. As fast as he was writing, you would think he would be caught up. I guess not. "How do you know Scott Manor?"

"We went to school together."

"That's it?"

"We have had sexual encounters before too."

"So you two used to date?"

"No, we just used to hang out and have sex sometimes."

"Mmhmm. Got it. So when was the last time you two were intimate?"

"I'm not sure really. I haven't seen him in a while."

"I see," he said, writing some more. "Why do you think he was following you?"

"I don't know. Probably because he's a fucking creep."

"A fucking creep. Got it," he said. I shook my head laughing. This guy was hilarious.

"Well, my theory is that he wants you. Maybe he misses you."

"So instead of picking up the phone like a normal person, he decides to turn into a stalker? Does that make any sense to you?"

"No, it doesn't, but in my line of work, I've heard it all. Maybe he just got obsessed with you and you were unaware."

"Maybe."

He got up and left the room. I was left alone. I pulled my cell phone out my shoe and texted my mother and told her where I was. She said just come there after I'm finished. I also texted Mario:

Me: what the hell is going on? Why were you trying to kill me earlier?

Mario: I wasn't. I was trying to save you

Me: save me from what?

Mario: that guy that was in the tinted out black van

I froze. How did he know about Scott?

Me: how did you know about that?

Mario: first off, I knew where you were the entire time. They were watching you and I was watching them.

Me: but why?

Mario: idk why. I was hoping you could answer that for me.

Me: we need to talk in person

Mario: wya?

Me: police station

Mario: texting me?

Me: my phone was in my shoe

Mario: I taught u too much LOL. how much longer you gonna be there?

Me: the detective said they would let me leave shortly

Mario: let me know when you are done and I will meet you

Me: ok

Mario: I love you, boo

Me: love you 2

The detective came back in and told me they were gonna hold Scott for more questioning. He gave me a brief rundown of the upcoming events and let me leave. I was relieved too. I felt like a criminal sitting in that damn interrogation room. Thought I was gonna die if I didn't get out of there fast enough. I called Mario and told him to meet me at the hotel because that's where I was headed. He said he would be there in ten minutes. It was gonna take me about twenty to get to him if I didn't speed. I didn't want to speed. I wanted to sit and collect my thoughts before seeing him. I drove the normal speed limit until I arrived back at the hotel. I parked my car in the garage and told him I was there. I got out and I saw him walk over to me. I hugged him tightly and his hug matched mine. I didn't want to let him go.

"Are you okay, Desiree?" he asked me.

"Yeah, I'm okay, Mario. I'm just scared, that's all."

"You don't need to be, Baby. I'm here to protect you. I'm here to protect our baby, Desiree."

"What about, Lexi?" I asked, pushing him away from me. I know he didn't think I forgot about that bitch.

"What about her?"

"Mario you had her in our bed. What the fuck you mean?"

Nymphopervtress

"I know I fucked up, Desiree. And I'm sorry. But I do love you, Baby and I wanna make it up to you."

"How the hell do you think you're gonna fix this? Please enlighten me."

"Well, I don't know. How about I buy you something? A new house?"

"Maybe. I don't know. But we do need to talk about the situation at hand."

"Okay, let's talk."

We went inside the hotel and I took him up to my room. We sat down and I took a deep breath.

"The guy that was following me was a friend of mine. Well, I thought he was anyway. We used to have sex a while back and I eventually stopped seeing him. That was when you and I had gotten more serious."

"When you say awhile back, how far back are we talking?"

"Six months."

"Six months? Desiree, it's going on damn near a fucking year since we've been messing with each other. So you mean to tell me you were fucking him in the beginning of our relationship?"

"Yeah, but it wasn't intentional. It was a mistake."

"A mistake, huh? You know what else was a mistake?"

"What?"

"Ever dealing with your trifling ass."

"Really, Mario? I made a mistake. I'm only human. You on the other hand went behind my back and was still seeing that bitch after you said you were done with her. Who is really in the wrong here? Because it damn sure ain't me."

He took a deep breath. He looked at me and my face was covered in tears. "Come here, Baby." I walked over to him and he held me. "Just let it all out, Boo. We both made some mistakes in the past but now we gotta look forward to the future. We have to, for the sake of our child. I love you, Desiree."

"I love you too, Mario."

"Cool. Now we can start fresh," he said, as he got my bags and stuff together.

"What are you doing?"

"I'm taking you home. Tomorrow morning, I wanna wake up next to you. Tomorrow, the day after, and the day after that. I wanna wake up next to you for the rest of my life. Promise me that you will."

"I promise."

Chapter Twenty-Six:
I Need Help

Ihad been tossing and turning every night for the past week, after the series of events that occurred. I thought about everything that has happened to me in the past year. From me and Jay, to me and Mario, to everything else. I could barely sleep. All together, I may have accumulated about five hours of sleep during the past seven days. This was an outrage. I had to talk to somebody about my problems and quick. I turned over to Mario. He was sleeping so peaceful. I watched as his chest rose and fell. I was so in love with this man but I just didn't know how to change my ways. I was afraid to settle for just one man. What if things didn't work out between us? Then what? I was gonna be assed out with no back-up plans. I didn't want to disturb him so I quietly got up out of bed and went over to my laptop.

I searched for therapists near me. It came up with over five hundred listings. I scanned through the listings until I fell upon one. Her name was Dr. Nicholson. She was a train ride away. I called and they told me I could come in at 10. It was already 9. I had to take a shower and get dressed. I ran around the room as quietly as possible so I wouldn't wake Mario. I grabbed my smart trip card and ran out the house. I made it outside just in time to catch the J bus. It dropped me off at Addison Road Metro Station. I paid my fare and waited for the train. The train came two minutes later. "Oh, God," I said when the doors opened. The train cars were all packed with morning commuters. I managed to squeeze into the middle of the second train car. I held my purse close to me so nobody could rob me.

People kept bumping one another as the train rocked back and forth. I kept feeling something on my ass. I turned and saw a lot of people behind me so I couldn't single one out. Whoever it was, boldly started rubbing on my ass and squeezing my left cheek. I just let it happen. It was feeling good as well as taking my mind off this horrible train ride. They cupped my pussy through my leggings and I moved my hips back and forth slowly. I looked around to make sure nobody was looking and I grabbed their hand. I used my other hand to reach around and place their hand inside the back of my leggings. They roughly played with my insides until I came. I heard the train operator announce that we were headed to L'Enfant Plaza. That was my stop.

I removed the stranger's hand from my pants and straightened up my attire. I got off the train when the doors opened like nothing had happened. I got to the elevator and a guy came up beside me and waited as well. It was odd that we were the only two waiting. Maybe everybody else was in a rush. The light signaled that the elevator had arrived. Finally. I thought to myself. He let me on first then followed. He pushed the button and I thanked him.

"You smell good," the guy said, out the blue.

"Thank you," I responded politely.

"You taste good, too."

I looked at him and he was licking his fingers. "How would you know that?"

"Because I just tasted it."

"Oh, so that was you playing with me on the train?"

"Mmhmm," he said proudly. "I thought maybe we could finish it."

"Oh yeah? Where?"

"We can go to the McDonald's right on the corner. They are always packed so they won't even notice us going into the bathroom."

"Let's go," I said. What the hell was I doing? I was supposed to be trying to fix the problem not adding more fire to it. But I went ahead anyway. There was no turning back from it now. We went through the side door and he was right. Everybody was here for their lunch break right now. We snuck into the women's bathroom and went into the big stall with the changing table.

He kissed my lips and my neck as I removed my coat and his. He pulled my shirt off and played with my titties. I took off my boots and my leggings. I left my panties on and he snatched them off, tearing them. He threw them on the floor and pulled his penis out. He kneeled on the floor and jerked it as he stretched my pussy with the other hand and enjoyed a second helping. He sat me on the baby changing station and stuck his dick inside me. He fucked me so damn hard and rough that the table had broken underneath of me. He grabbed me in mid-air. He put me on the floor and stretched his coat out on the floor.

I laid down atop the coat and he got back inside of me. I could feel a little bit of the floor under my butt and it was so cold. I put my legs up in the air so he could get in deeper. I didn't even notice I was getting pushed into the corner as he fucked me. Now I really couldn't go nowhere. I felt his warm semen shoot up inside of me. As much as it was, I know my baby got a little bit of it too. I grabbed some tissue and cleaned myself up. I reached in my purse and got some of my feminine wipes. I handed him a couple to clean himself and I took out two. Once I was finished, I put my clothes and everything else back on. I was headed out the bathroom when he stopped me.

"Hey, what's your name?"

"Doesn't matter."

"My name is Xavier."

"And?"

"Can I have your number?"

"No."

"Can I see you again?"

"Not a chance." I walked out the bathroom. I had to hurry across the street. It was ten minutes after ten and I was late for my appointment. I jogged to the building. When I stepped into the building, I walked straight to the receptionist desk. "Hi, I'm here to see Dr. Nicholson."

"You can take the elevator up to the fifth floor."

"Thank you." I walked over to the bank of elevators and got on the first one that came. I hit the fifth floor button and waited for the elevator. When the doors opened, a group of people got off and I got on. I was all alone. I was nervous as I rode the elevator. What kind of questions were she gonna ask me? What if she asked too many questions? I wasn't prepared for this. I stepped off the elevator when I got to the fifth floor. I was getting ready to head back on it when someone called my name.

"You must be, Desiree Logan."

I turned and saw a beautiful black woman standing before me. "Yes I am."

"Nice to meet. I'm Dr. Nicholson. Or you can call me Janet."

"Nice to meet you."

"You can follow me to my office."

"Okay." I walked closely behind her. I observed her from behind and she was the total package. She had a beautiful face, a beautiful smile, nice round ass, and big breasts. They were probably as big as mine if not bigger. We got to her office and we sat down.

"So what brings you in to see me today, Desiree?"

"Well, I have been going through a lot in this past year. And I do mean a lot."

"Like what?" she asked, pulling out a memo pad to write on.

"Well, like my sex life. It's been ridiculous."

"Is that a good thing or bad thing?"

"Both. I have had more than two partners."

"That's not really a lot."

"You didn't let me finish. I have had sex with my current boyfriend, my ex-boyfriend, all three of my best friends, even strangers. I just had sex with somebody in the McDonald's bathroom on the corner. I need help," I said, crying into my hands.

"Really? That's uncanny. Wait a minute. You said you just had sex in a public restroom?"

"Yes," I said, sniffling.

"How is that even possible?"

"Anything is possible when you set your mind to something."

"I guess you're right. Now let's talk about your boyfriend. Does he know what's going on?"

"No. Mario doesn't know anything. He only knows about the guy that tried to kill me."

"Okay. Let's back up some more. Tell me a little more about that situation." I ran down everything about the incident with Scott and how it led up to that. I know I was overwhelming her with my outlandish ways. "Wow, that's crazy."

"Yeah, I know," I responded. "And it doesn't help the fact that I'm pregnant."

"You are? How far along are you?"

"I'm three months now."

"Well, congratulations. How do you and Mario feel about having your first baby?"

"We are both excited. I think he is more excited than I am."

"Why do you think that?"

"Because I'm still a little traumatized from my previous pregnancy."

"How long ago were you pregnant?"

"About six months ago. It was horrible. I lost my baby because I was raped by some guy I met on Tagged. He took me to an abandoned building and him and his friends all ganged up on me. I miscarried and it's been haunting me ever since. I didn't even know who my child's father was. So in a way, it saved me from humiliation."

"I see."

"But the impact it had on my life was crazy. When I thought about it, it turned me on."

"It turned you on?"

"Yes, and then I ended up having a foursome with my boyfriend and my two female best friends. It was an enjoyable experience," I said with a smile.

"How did you feel seeing your boyfriend having sex with your friends?"

"Well, it was only one. The other one is gay. But it was cool. Like I said, I had fun. He caught us having sex and he joined in instead of getting mad. And then there was another time I had had sex with these two guys that worked at the grocery store. We had sex there."

"How did you have sex in the grocery store? In the bathroom?"

"No. In the walk-in freezer in the produce section. The guy and I were having sex with a cucumber and then he started penetrating me. His boss caught us and I asked him to join in."

"Do you feel any guilt for what you are doing?"

"Not at all."

"Do you at least use protection with these people?"

"Not all the time."

"Have you ever had a sexually transmitted disease?"

"Yes, but that didn't stop me from feeding my cravings."

"I am gonna be here for you, Desiree."

"What is that supposed to mean?"

"You need help."

Chapter Twenty-Seven:
Nymphopervtress

⁓

It's been going on six months now since I started seeing Dr. Nicholson. She said I have been showing little progress. I still had my urges unfortunately. They were getting more and more out of control because of my pregnancy. I walked into her office as I usually did.

"How are you feeling, Desiree?" she asked, handing me a bottle of water.

"I'm okay I guess."

"You don't sound too sure. What's going on?"

"Well, I need to have sex and a lot of it."

"Your fiancé isn't giving you any?"

"Yeah he is, but it's not enough. I need more. I need more partners. Hell I wish I could get more than one at one time," I said, sounding frustrated. She disregarded everything I just ranted about. She was quickly writing.

"I have been going over your papers and I have come up with a diagnosis for you."

"Which is what?"

"Hyper sexuality."

"Come again. What is that?"

"The medical definition for someone that suffers from hyper sexuality is someone who has frequent or sudden sexual urges or sexual activity. In other words, a nymphomaniac. And since you're a woman, it's another word for you."

"Which is what?"

"Nymphopervtress."

"But what does all of this mean?"

"It just means that you love to have sex. And when your body craves it, you're gonna go out and get that craving taken care of by any means necessary."

"So in other words, I'm a hoe?"

"I didn't say that."

"You don't have to. You implied it," I said, standing up and yelling. "I don't wanna hear this shit. I'm out of here." I grabbed my things and headed for the door.

"Where are you gonna go, Desiree? You can't run from this illness."

"Yes I can. I can stop whenever I want to."

"It's not that simple, Desiree."

"How do you know?"

"Because I'm just like you."

I looked at her. She wouldn't even look at me. She just turned and walked back over to the sofa. I walked back over and sat beside her.

"I found out about this condition when I was 25. I didn't know how to control it. It ruined my marriage, my relationships with friends, my job, everything. By the time I was 30, I was a single mom of two children. Every night while my kids slept, I would sneak a different person into the house. I would get what I wanted and have them gone by sunrise. I ended up getting help eventually, but it took me too long. I had gotten caught at work having sex with one of the underage interns. I had to do six months in jail and I went through an ugly custody battle. Now at the age of 50, I'm glad to say I'm free. I have my kids' back and my family and I are back speaking for the most part. Moral of the story is get help while it's being offered. Stop it before it's too late for you."

Her story had brought me to tears. I didn't want to end up like that. In my head, I was doing far more worse than she was. I couldn't control it nor did I want to. But I had to do it. If not for myself, for the sake of my child. "How do I go about doing this?"

"First off, you have to come to therapy at least once a week. I'm gonna put you on medication."

"What kind of medication?" I asked cutting her off. "Is it gonna hurt the baby?"

"No, it's perfectly fine, Desiree. It's just meds that will keep your sexual urges under control. It's called Zoloft and I can assure you that it works very effectively. I have been taking it for years and I love it."

"Does that mean I'm not gonna want to have sex anymore?"

"No, it just means that your hormones won't be sky-high like normally. It's especially good for you to take during your pregnancy. During this phase in your life, your hormones are higher than ever before."

"Why can't I just try this without the medicine?"

"You can, but it's not gonna work. You have an illness and you're not gonna be able to stop it. No matter what happens in your life, everything plays out into your sexual relationships. Like for example, not to bring this up, but when you got raped, you were scared and it traumatized you when it happened. And now you find it exciting and it gives you a rush every time you think about it. That's a problem."

"How did I catch it?" I asked her with teary eyes.

"It's not something that you can catch from anywhere. It just happens.

It is yet to be scientifically proven how individuals get this disorder. "Here," she said handing me a bottle of pills. "I already had your prescription filled for to-day."

"Thanks," I said, taking it from her. I just looked at the bottle.

"I want you to take one of these every morning, during or after breakfast. You can actually take it right after your prenatal vitamin.

I shook my head in disbelief. "What do I do now?"

"Go home and tell your Mario what's going on."

****

I told Mario to hurry and get home because it was urgent. He said he was on the way. I went over what I was gonna say and how I was gonna say it in my head. I told Dr. Nicholson to give me a copy of the diagnosis so I could show it to Mario. It was just in case he didn't believe me. In a way I knew he wasn't going to. I was sitting in the living when I heard Mario pull into the driveway. I turned on the TV and pretended like I was watching it the entire time when he walked in.

"Hey, Baby. What's going on?" he asked, as he rushed over to me and sat down.

"I need to talk to you, Mario."

"That's the urgency? Because you needed to talk?"

"Yes."

"Is it about the baby, Desiree?" he asked, placing a hand on my stomach. I took his hand off my belly and held it.

"The baby is fine, Mario. This is about me."

"So what's going on?"

"I'm sick, Mario. I have an illness."

"Like AIDS or something?"

"No, not anything like that. I mean a mental illness."

He threw his head back in laughter. "A mental illness? Who in the hell told you that?"

"Well, I have been seeing this therapist and-"

"A therapist? I don't believe this shit. What the hell are you going to a therapist for? I'm your man. I'm always here to listen and help."

"But you can't help me with this. I was diagnosed with hyper sexuality."

"What the fuck is that?"

"It's a disorder that causes people to have frequent and sudden sexual urges and want to participate in sexual activities. Maybe I ought to start from

Nymphopervtress

the beginning."

"Yeah, maybe you should," he said, propping his feet up on the table. And leaning back on the chair. I had his undivided attention now.

I told him the whole story. Everything. Every person I messaged. Every dick I sucked or pussy I ate. I told him the real story behind the rape. I let it all out; including the episode I had two months ago in the McDonald's bathroom. When I eventually finished my story, I was in tears. I looked over to him and he wore a stoned face.

"Well?"

"Well what, Desiree?"

"Do you have anything to say?"

"As far as what? About my fiancé being a whore?"

"I'm not a whore, Mario," I said. The tears started to well up in my eyes again.

"Then what the fuck are you then, Desiree?" he asked, standing up over top of me. "You were the reason I had caught an STD. Your ass was the reason why you got raped. Your ass was even the reason why I lost my first child," he said. He stopped in mid turn. "Or was that even my child?"

"I don't know, Mario. I don't know if that was your baby or not."

"This is fucking crazy."

I grabbed his arm. "I need you, Baby. Please. I need you to help me get through this. You said you would always be here for me and the baby."

"Yeah, I did say that. But that was before I found out everything that you did behind my back. And then having the nerve to flip the fuck out on me when I did wrong. That's fucked up, Desiree, and you know it. I'm gonna be there for my baby no doubt. I can promise you that. But as far as you go, I can't deal with this right now."

"Mario, please," I begged. I dropped to my knees and held onto his leg so he couldn't move.

"Desiree, let me go!" he yelled and shook me off his leg. "I fucking hate you! I hate everything that you are. Your ass is dead to me." He went out the door and slammed it. He slammed the door so hard the little window broke at the top of the door."

I sat there crying in the middle of the floor. I laid down in a fetal position on the hardwood floor and cried myself to sleep with only one thing on my mind: I was dead to Mario.

Nymphopervtress

Chapter Twenty-Eight:
Intervention

It has been days since I had heard anything from Mario. I have been trying to reach out to him but nothing worked. I sent him the address for how to get to Dr. Nicholson's office. I wanted him to be there with me alongside my family and friends during my intervention. I needed all the support I could get.

We all arrived at the therapy office a quarter to 11. I told my mom and my friends what was going on and what was going to happen before Dr. Nicholson did. I didn't see Mario's car anywhere. I guess he wasn't gonna come. We headed up to the fifth floor.

"Hey, Dr. Nicholson," I said, as I walked into her office.

"How are you feeling, Desiree?" she asked, giving me a hug.

"I feel confident."

"That's a good word to use."

"I do. I feel like I'm ready to change my life over for the better. Especially for my baby girl."

"A girl?"

"Yes."

"I'm so happy for you," she said, giving me another hug. "Why don't you introduce me to everyone?"

I pointed to each person as I gave the introduction. "This is my mom, Denise; my sister, Monet, and my best friends, Shannon and Jessica."

"Where is Mario, Desiree?"

"I'm right here." We all turned around to see Mario standing in the doorway. "Sorry I'm late, Doc.

"No, no, it's perfectly fine. We haven't even started yet."

He walked over to me and held my hands. "I know I was being an asshole the other day when you told me all of what was going on. I apologize for being so mean and disrespectful to you, Baby. I love you and I'm gonna help you get through this. And do you know why?"

"Because we're a team," I said, with tears suddenly streaming down my cheeks.

"Not only that. Because we are gonna be parents to a beautiful baby girl soon. She needs us. She needs you and so do I. You're my ride or die."

"Until the day we die, Baby." He kissed me and hugged me like he didn't wanna let me go.

"Well, that was one hell of an introduction. Now let's get down to the curing process. Shall we?" Dr. Nicholson said, sitting down in her chair.

We all listened attentively as she told everyone about my diagnosis and what they could do to help me and what all I could do for myself. We were there for about two hours before everything was all said and done.

****

We were finally back at me and Mario's house. Never in a million years would I have thought my mind could be on anything other than sex. Because of those pills, I have been extremely calm. Whenever Mario and I had sex now, I was perfectly satisfied. There was no more sneaking around. I deleted my Tagged page, POF, Twitter, and even Facebook. I didn't want to have no unintended slip-ups while I was on my road to recovery.

Mario was rubbing my feet and we were just relaxing.

"So, Babe, tell me something."

"What's up?" I asked.

"How long has this been going on? Your sexual addiction."

"Well, I started having these urges since I was 14. I didn't think nothing of it because I thought it was normal. So I never questioned it or asked questions."

"Oh. What do you think would have happened if you found out sooner?"

"I don't know. I always wonder that though. If I did, I may not have ever met you," I said, looking at him.

"I think you would have still found me. It was fate. We were meant to be together, Baby."

"That's good to know."

I felt a sharp pain in my stomach and I jumped up. "What's the matter, Boo?" Mario asked as he jumped up with me.

"I think I'm having contractions. Ahh," I said, grabbing my stomach. "I think it's time."

"Oh shit," he said, running around. "Where's your hospital bag?"

"It's in the car already."

"Okay good. I'm gonna go get the car and you wait right here."

"Okay, Baby. Hurry up. These damn contractions are hurting like hell."

"Okay, okay. I'm going." He grabbed his phone and car keys and ran to the garage. I managed to make it to the front door and wait for him. I saw him back out the driveway and he drove off. "Ain't this some shit?" I said aloud. I dialed his number and he picked up. "Mario if you don't get your black ass back here and get my fat ass!"

"Oh shit. My bad, Desiree. I'm coming now." I walked out to the sidewalk where I knew he would see me. I was in too much pain to be left again. And I was definitely in too much damn pain to wait for them slow ass paramedics. I called my mom and told her we were headed to Prince George's Community Hospital in Cheverly. She told me she and my sister would be there. I called my friends and they too were on their way.

*****

"Push, Baby, push," Mario yelled at me. I was in so much pain from them damn contractions but I refused the epidural. Now I was in here suffering, trying to do natural birth.

I pushed and pushed and pushed. This little girl was being so goddamn stubborn. "Aahhh," I screamed louder.

"I can see the head. Oh wow, look at all that hair," Dr. Habib said. "One more strong push should do it, Desiree." I did one more long push and didn't stop until I felt her entire body come out. My pussy was hurting and it felt like I had just given birth to a baby elephant. Mario cut the umbilical cord and held up our baby girl. She was beautiful and a little chunky.

I watched as the nurses cleaned her up and weighed her. She was seven pounds and three ounces. She had a head full of curly hair that made her look like a little doll baby. They wrapped her in a baby blanket and handed her to me. "Hello, little baby. I'm your mommy and that's your daddy," I said, pointing to Mario. My family and friends came in the room to see the adorable bundle of joy that Mario and I had created.

"What's her name?" my little sister asked.

I looked over to Mario. "What are we gonna name her, Hun?"

He rubbed his beard and snapped his fingers when it came to him.

"Zaniyah Alesia Davis."

Epilogue

My healing process over this past year has been a success. Mario and I have recently exchanged vows. Zaniyah is getting bigger and getting ready to celebrate her first birthday this weekend. Nothing could possibly go wrong. It was like I was living in a fairytale. I had my knight in shining armor by my side and I had my little princess who made living worthwhile.

Dr. Nicholson was still around as well. She has been the best therapist and have come to be someone I could talk to on an every other day basis. She liked for me to check-in and I had no problem with that. My mom and my sister were a big help too, surprisingly. My sister practically moved into our house so she could be with her niece all the time. I didn't have a problem with it and neither did Mario. It gave us a lot of time to take care of business and make sure our family was taken care of.

I'm so proud of myself for reaching out for help. I saw that I had a problem and I got it taken care of before it took over my life and ruined it. I haven't even thought about another guy or anything since I had been going to therapy. I guess those doctors really know how to do their jobs. If I could press the rewind button on my life and have it turn out differently, I wouldn't. I was just lucky to be living my life with my daughter and my husband as Mrs. Desiree Michelle Davis.

www.ingramcontent.com/pod-product-compliance
Lightning Source LLC
Chambersburg PA
CBHW071916220626
47052CB00002B/373